****

TIDES INN

DUOLOGY

****

Tides Inn – Camaraderie Is Deadly
Tides Inn – Shock From the Deep

Thanks to Barbara, Janet, and Sandy for their tough love editing.
Thanks to Sally for her support and patience.

....

Book One
Camaraderie is Deadly

Book Two
Shock From The Deep

....

[Type here]

A TIDES INN MYSTERY

Book 1

CAMARADERIE IS DEADLY

Bill Wilke

[Type here]

<u>CAMARADERIE IS DEADLY -</u>

Chapter One
The Crime

The howling, frigid, nor'easter raced across the bay, whipping the water into a frenzy. Waves explode, angrily lashing out at the rugged embankments of a narrow, rocky, jutting peninsula. On the surface of the receding water, trapped in the eddies along the rock, phosphorous silver froth swirls and shimmers eerily in the bright moonlight. Anchored firmly at the end of this neck-of-land stood a picturesque, weather-beaten building, the 'Tides Inn'. The scene was one of beauty, but definitely not a night to be outside. - - - But inside, in a nice, cozy, warm pub, ah, now that was a different story.

*   *   *

The dart was straight and true.

"Bulls-eye!", exclaimed Derek Finnegan, whose receding brown hairline, betrayed his forty years of age.

"Yeah, but you need a red one." answered Bunny Chase, in her thirties, American, blonde, with a soft. silky voice, who had retained her ex-showgirl figure.

"It IS in the red," argued Derek.

Bunny and Carole Coxton, short, heavy set, peeking out through dark rooted stringy bleached blond hair, walked side by side toward the dartboard.

"It's in the black." returned Bunny.

Carole, "Red."

Bunny, confidence waning, "Bla-c-k."

Carole, now standing directly in front of the board, reached up, bent the dart sideways, revealing that the dart was indeed on the black side of the wire. She adamantly pointed, "Come look at it. Look and weep."

Bunny stopped just in front of the dartboard.

Bunny then leaned over cringing, "Dammit! Dammit! Ian. It is in the red."

"Yes!" exuded Derek while doing a little dance and thrusting his fist forward.

"Dammit. Dammit. Dammit." echoed Ian O'Brien, also in his forties, red hair, speaking in an unmistakable Irish brogue, confirming his nationality of birth.

Carole skipped over to Derek and jumped up in front of him. Derek jumped up to meet her. They chest bumped.

Carole celebrated, "Dead-eye Derek!"

This lively banter flowed from a spirited dart game at the Tides Inn, a one-of-a-kind, popular inn, pleasingly positioned on the scenic English North Sea coast of Yorkshire, in the quaint little fishing village of Hopkins Bay.

The dart throwing group was the "regulars" that were "tide killing". Their interest at the moment was in both the dart game and in the football match on the telly between Manchester United and Arsenal. Those taking part in both activities were vocal and split in loyalties.

With the completion of the dart game, the four players moved to a table adjacent to the dartboard area with their pints. A large 'telly' over the bar was showing the British football match. In the corner, lying on a chair, on a big, soft pillow was Mimi, Bunny's fluffy, snow-white, miniature, French Poodle. This was

Mimi's throne when Bunny was playing darts. Bunny picked Mimi up and cradled her in an over-the-shoulder front carrier.

"Gavin, another round," said the bull's eye thrower, Derek Finnegan. He then turned and looked at Ian Finch. "Losers are buying."

"Right Ian?" needled Carole.

"That was just plain luck," said Bunny Chase, Ian's partner.

"Yeah. Ye had a wee bit of luck there mates." Added Ian.

"Luck! You're confusing luck with skill aren't you?" responded Derek.

"Oh, come, on give me a break. We whomped you," responded Carole "Quit your crying."

Gavin Roche, acknowledged, the request, "Drinks coming right up."

Gavin was the owner of the Inn, rugged looking, well built, with a closely trimmed black beard and the looks of a man who had been around the sea all his life, which he had. He walked over behind the bar, drew the four pints from an ornate, brass collection of taps, and then carried them over to the competitors' table. Then moving over to the fireplace, he drove a poker several times into a bright red bed of coals. Roaring flames immediately obeyed and exploded into action. After placing three more logs on the fire, he returned behind the bar and started drawing a pint for a Middle Eastern looking man standing at the bar.

"I haven't seen you in here before," commented the man standing next to the man.

"I'm staying at the Inn here for a couple of days."

Gavin, who had checked Ali Ahmed into a room at the pub a short time before, arrived with the pint and said, "Hamish, this is Mr. Ali Ahmed. Mr. Ahmed, Dr. Hamish Brindley is our retired village doctor. Just about every person in this village under 40 was delivered by Dr. Brindley."

"That's quite a record, Dr. Brindley', said Ali. "Was it tough to retire?"

Gavin interjected, "Oh, he still gets called in to help his replacement Dr. King,".

"Yeah, more times than I would like." Then Dr. Brindley, in his seventies, distinguished grey hair and distinguished voice asked Ali, "What brings you to Hopkins Bay?"

"Selling drugs." Then while looking smug at the reaction his statement roused, he added, "I'm a pharmaceutical salesman."

"Well, glad you explained that," grinned Dr. Brindley.

"This is a fascinating place," said Ali, looking around.

"Well, we're proud of it. Feel it is unique," said Gavin. "The building was once a lighthouse. The light tower was removed long ago, but the building is still considered a landmark. I'm slightly biased, but I think it provides the perfect ambiance."

"I certainly agree. I like it. But isn't it a problem to be cut-off from the outside world, like right now."

"Yeah, we're only a hundred feet away from the homeland, but with this high tide it could be a hundred miles," said Gavin.

"What about when there is an emergency?"

"Well, that could be a problem," answered Gavin. "But so far that has never happened. We just have to cross our fingers that it never will."

"Amazing," said Ali.

"Sometimes," stated Gavin, "when the tide comes in, the sea covers the pathway and I have a captive audience. But very few of my customers complain. I keep the drinks coming, even past closing hours."

"Don't the authorities have a problem with that?" asked Ali.

"Nope. We are off the beaten track. The authorities have never enforced closing hours. They make an exception in our case," said Gavin.

"Plus," said Dr. Brindley with a chuckle, "our local law enforcer, Police Sergeant Reggie Duke, is usually one of us trapped, and believe me, he is not one to go thirsty."

"He is sort of a rebel. Marches to his own drummer. And since we are so far off the beaten track, he can make his own rules," said Gavin.

Brinkley added, "And he is a reliable law officer. If there is ever a problem, Reggie is the one you want to call. Has a lot of respect from the locals."

"As for the closing of the ramp, the inaccessible times are predictable," added Gavin. "The times for high and low tide are posted, so everyone knows when they usually can and can't get out and can plan for it. Actually sometimes we can still cross at high tide. So you never completely know for sure."

"Even with this time schedule, the depth of the water must still vary. How do people know when the water level is low enough to be safe or not?" asked Ali.

"When the water rises and approaches the top of the walkway, an alarm sounds, and five minutes later a barrier gate closes at both ends of the path," explained Gavin. "The action works in reverse as the tide goes out."

Ali pointed toward the other side of the room. Located on a heavy wooden table was a large cylindrical glass aquarium. A full replica of a miniature diver in a diving suit floated on top with a dozen or so goldfish swimming in the water. A TV screen hung above and behind it. "What's with that tank and the miniature diver? I suspect it has something to do with the tide."

"Gavin answered, "The miniature diver we call "Ole' Pete." Ole' Pete' floats up and down in the tank with the tide. When the water approaches the top of the walk, he rises rapidly to the top of the tank. And then sinks to the bottom when the water reaches the top of the walkway on its way down.

"Wow, that is amazing."

Gavin continued, "Each time he goes up or down, eerie flashing lights flood the tank and trumpets blare."

"What a production. That is really clever. But those poor fish. They never get a break. Don't they ever complain?"

Haven't had one complain yet." responded Gavin.

Ali chuckles. "How does Ole' Pete know when to do all this?"

Gavin answered, "I have no idea. The whole alarm system is just another endeavor of our resident inventor, Derek Finnegan."

"That is truly amazing. Who did you say invented it?"

"Derek Finnegan. He just happens to be over there throwing darts. You will have to ask him about the details."

Dr. Brindley added, "And what's amazing is that the whole automatic system of warnings and barriers is so simple. The whole setup is activated by a float, one that you will find in any loo."

Dr. Brindley continued, "You should have been here a couple of years ago. Access was really tricky. There was no established walkway, so to go back and forth when the tide was out, everyone had to tip-toe around tide pools. Now, let me tell you, that was a challenge. But last year, Gavin built up the rocks and improved the footpath so that now you don't have to take your life in your hands to imbibe one of his libations."

"This place is truly impressive," said Ali, taking a sip and panning the room.

"Yes, we all love our pub. There is a whole lot of camaraderie here," said Brindley.

"I can see that," said Ali as he continued looking around the room.

The interior was fashioned in rock and warm, dark-polished wood paneling. Around the perimeter of the room, stuffed chairs, welcoming and restful, helped the occupants pass the tide-wait in complete comfort. Dominating the far side of the room was a large fireplace with a heavy wood mantle. And as usual, after Gavin's attention, the fireplace now housed a roaring monstrous fire with a big mound of black fur stretched out in front. This was Rosko, the house dog, a big, hairy, black Newfoundland.

Because of tonight's rough weather, it looked like a long time before any exit was going to be possible. But judging by the mood of those present, this entrapment was more than welcomed.

"By the way, you may want to talk to Carole Coxton," said Dr. Brindley, as he pointed to Carole in the dart area. Carole was just letting loose a practice dart. "She owns her own chemist shop in town, 'Care-For-You-Chemists'."

"Yes, I recognize the name. It's one of the shops I have on my list. I will be sure to talk with her."

"Hey, ole man," Ian called from across the room to Giles Chase, a heavy-set, 65 year old import/exporter who was married to the much younger dart player, Bunny. Giles was seated in a cozy corner across from the bar reading a book. He was quite a bit older than Bunny, and this difference in age was the subject of many snide comments. Giles was scowling. Of course. Giles always scowled. The surrounding coziness was completely wasted on him. On a table next to him rested his pint of ale and a flower vase. A seascape and a small window were situated on the wall behind him.

"Hey, ole man," Ian repeated after not getting a response the first time. "Ye want ta join Bunny and take on the lucky whiners, I mean winners?" This comment earned a jab to the back of the ribs from Carole.

A barely audible grunt stemmed from Giles as he continued absorbed in his book.

"I take that as a no," said Ian, then adding under his breath, "You ole goat. You don't' deserve Bunny. She has ta get free of him. One these days, someone is going to bash his cranium, mark my word."

Carole overheard him. "Wow, that was pretty powerful."

"Just a good ole Irish saying that pretty well fits the occasion."

Giles verified his answer with another low grunt.

Bunny carried her very shapely ex-show girl body over to her husband, leaned over, displaying a little more than should have been displayed, and gave him a buss on the cheek. "Oh, don't be such a grump, Giles,"

He looked up at her. "I'm perfectly happy here, thank you. Go do your thing."

Bunny glided back to the bar.

"Okay, what say we do it again?" said Ian addressing Bunny. "I think it's time we put the kibosh on these guys. What say old girl?"

"Hold on a minute. Got to pet my good luck charm," said Derek as he strolled over and gave Rosko a pat on the head. This triggered a barely cracked open eyelid and an ever so slight movement of one stretched-out paw.

"Boy, I have never seen him that excited about your dart game before, Derek," said Carole.

The four players gathered; the banter and the game began again. Giles drained his pint and went to the bar next to Brindley to get a refill. "Gavin, my usual. And make sure you get it right this time.

"What?"

"That one," said Giles as he pointed to the returned glass, "wasn't my usual."

"What're you talking about, Giles." Then motioning to the glass, he was presently drawing, he said, "That last one was the same as this one. It was your usual. Did it taste bad? Did it taste like it had gone off?"

"Nope. I just know from the taste it was not my beer."

"If you didn't like it, why didn't you bring it back?"

"I know what my beer tastes like. . . And this," he again pointed at the glass, "was not my beer."

Giles watched the pouring operation intently. When Gavin finished, he abruptly grabbed the newly filled glass, causing a slight spilling of beer. With some beer dribbling down the side of the glass, he returned to his chair, completely ignoring Gavin.

Brindley, who observed the whole operation, just shook his head, then looked at Gavin, who was wiping up the spill. "The way he was watching you. That boy has some big trust issues."

Several minutes later, the room erupted as Arsenal scored a goal. Everyone moved to the bar for a closer look.

"Bloody hell! Did ya see that? What a kick," exclaimed Ian.

"What do you mean, 'what a kick'? Did you see the way it ricocheted off Barstone's foot? Pure, blind luck. Blind luck, dammit!" grumbled Derek.

"Talk about a fluke," agreed Carole. "Watch the replay."

Giles got up and took a trip to the WC. As he returned, Ian called out to him, "Giles, did ya see that goal?"

"Nope, don't really care."

Ian shrugged his shoulders and returned his attention to the telly. Rosko struggled to his feet, and as Giles sat down, Rosko promptly plopped on the floor next to his feet.

"Hey, what have you got going with Rosko there, Giles? Never saw him show any interest in you before," said Derek.

This again received a low grunt from Giles. "It may surprise you, but dogs like me." He then bent over and ran his fingers over Rosko's head.

"Well, this is certainly a new-found relationship," answered Derek. Then added under his breath, "Rosko is about the only one around here that likes the old bugger."

The dart game began again, and the players returned to splitting their attention between the dart game and the football match.

Chapter Two
Oh-Oh Poor Giles

H—o—w—l ! H—o—w—l !! A commotion from Rosko in the corner.

"Rosko, what on earth has gotten into you?" asked Gavin.

Then suddenly, Giles stood up, "Gavin, you really screwed up again. That beer tastes terrible! That is not mine. This tastes even worse than the one before."

Everyone stopped and looked at him.

Suddenly **Giles's head flew back.** He gasped, doubled over, and fell face first. Dr. Brindley dashed to the prostrate body and quickly turned him over on his back. Kneeling next to him, he grabbed his wrist, felt around his neck. "No pulse," he muttered under his breath. He quickly leaned over to start mouth-to-mouth resuscitation, but immediately popped back up. He placed the palms of his hands on Giles chest, alternately pushing and releasing. Nothing. He remained there on his knees staring at Giles. Finally, he slowly stood up. Still staring at Giles, he said in low voice, "He's dead."

"NO! NO! OH NO!" screamed Bunny, throwing herself across the body, her long black, silky hair flowing over to the floor.

"I knew it. I knew that the ole bugger's disposition was goin' to bring on a coronary," said Ian.

"Nope," said Dr. Brindley. "It wasn't a heart attack."

"What!" exclaimed Ian.

"Then what was it?" asked Gavin.

"He's been poisoned."

"Poisoned?" echoed from several lips in disbelief. "Poisoned?"

"I don't believe it," stated Derek.

"I'm afraid so."

"GILES NO! NO!" Bunny continually screamed.

"What makes you think he's been poisoned?" asked Carole.

"From the smell."

"The smell?" asked Gavin.

"Yes. When I knelt to perform mouth-to-mouth, there was a distinct smell of almond. And as quick as he died, I'm sure it was cyanide poisoning."

The room was deathly quiet. . . Except for Bunny quietly sobbing, as Carole buried her face into Derek's chest.

Dr. Brindley issued a big sigh. "Guess I better call Reggie." He walked to the bar and grabbed the phone.

A female voice answered the phone. "Hopkin's Bay Police Department. Constable Thompkins speaking."

"Oh, hello, Constable Thompkins. This is Dr. Brindley. Is Reggie in?" Constable Thompkins was in her thirties, young, blonde, slim, attractive, headstrong.

"No, he's off this evening. Can I help you?"

"Well, I really need to talk to Reggie."

"I'm sorry, Police Sergeant Duke is off duty. If you need anything right now, you're stuck with me."

"Dammit! Can you call him? This is really of great urgency."

A pause. Constable Thompkins firmly replied, "Nope, he gave specific orders not to be disturbed."

"I think he would be of a different mind if he knew the situation."

"And what is the situation?"

"We have had an incident here at the Tides."

"Yes. What kind of an incident?"

"A man has been poisoned."

There was another short pause. "Yes, Dr. Brindley, murder you say."

"Poisoned is what I said, but you can call it murder if you want." Brindley added under his breath, "This is going to be one stupid process until we can get a hold of Reggie."

"What happened?"

"One of the Inn's patrons, Giles Chase, has gotten a hold of a poisoned drink."

"Are you sure it was poison?"

"YES, I'm sure! I'm a doctor. You better get over here as soon as you can."

"Be right there. Don't touch anything."

Dr. Brindley covered the mouthpiece of the phone and said to the others, "She said 'don't touch anything'. How original. We know where she got her training."

"My first guess would be from Agatha Christie," said Derek.

Gavin walked behind the bar and picked up the tide report. "Hamish, it'll be another hour before the tide is out enough for the gates to open. And, there might be even more of a problem right now with the surf banging away out there."

Dr. Brindley relayed this information to the Constable and recommended she wait an hour or so before attempting to cross the walkway.

"Well, for a while now the wind has died down. Maybe the sea has calmed down a little with it. You can override the automatic opening and closing of the gates, can't you?"

"Yeah, but I'm looking out the window at the walkway. There is no way someone could cross over right now. The water's deep and the waves are heavy. Doesn't look like the sea has settled much."

"Do you think that hour estimate is accurate?" asked Thompkins.

Dr. Brindley conveyed the Constable's question to Gavin.

"I would say that an hour sounds pretty reasonable."

This was relayed back to the Constable.

She responded, "I'll leave immediately. Is there any way that I can contact you from the end of the ramp?"

"We have an intercom."

"Good, I'll give you a call."

"Okay, we'll be looking for you. But be careful. Take a good look at the surf. A big wave could knock you off the walkway before you know what hit you."

"I'll be careful."

"Oh, and can you alert the paramedics. There's no urgency. I'll give them a call when they can cross."

He returned to the group. "Constable Thompkins will be here when the water is down enough. She wants everybody to leave the crime area. She refused to call Reggie. Looks like she wants to take charge. I'm afraid that Reggie was right about her. Oh well, guess we'd better do what she says."

Everyone moved to the bar except Bunny who remained lying across the body sobbing and Carole who had moved to her side.

Brindley asked Gavin, "Do you have something to cover the body?"

Gavin went to a cabinet alongside the side wall and returned with a big tablecloth, and gently covered the body. He then returned to the bar, filled everybody's pint glass and added a shot of whisky in front of each pint. The whisky, to a glass quickly disappeared.

Chapter Three
Investigation / Conflict

"Constable Thompkins here. Open the gates."

"Are you sure you can handle the walkway? It's been only forty minutes. The surf still looks pretty tough," answered Gavin over the intercom.

"I'm looking at your depth gauges down the walkway. It looks like it's only a little over a foot deep. There're still a few nasty waves, but I'll hang on. I'm on my way."

She paused a few moments though. She knew she was going to be in the spotlight. There had been many doubts and snide remarks from many people about having a woman on the police force. And the most outspoken critic was her boss, Reggie Duke. He complained, far and wide, to all who would listen, especially while hoisting a pint at the Tides Inn, about having a women constable foisted upon him by the village fathers. This was on top of the "newcomer" syndrome she was already experiencing, that was inherent in being a stranger in a new village. With all of this going on, this was going to be her first major test. She had a lot to prove. . . She took a deep breath.

Reaching down, she removed her shoes, placed them in her shoulder bag, and rolled up the pants legs of her uniform. After a short pause, the gates creaked open. She began to wade through the water, becoming more apprehensive with each step. The path was well marked with four-foot-high metal posts, connected by a chain, which she gripped tightly, advancing hand over hand, while water swirled around her shins. Blasts from errant violent waves produced a few anxious moments.

As Gavin watched apprehensively from the end of the path, the tall, slim Dawn Thompkins inched her way toward him. Her glamorous looks made her appear out of place as a constable. The incoming waves smacked at her legs; the receding water sucked at her ankles. She had almost reached the end when a particularly strong wave broadsided her. Luckily, she was right at a post. She hung on tightly. The powerful wave had been defied. She had held her ground. But as it continued receding on over the walk, the powerful suction from the departing water jerked one foot out from under her. The wave had not surrendered yet. She applied a death grip on the post. Veins rose on the back of her hands. She dug desperately into the walk's rocky surface with her other foot trying to keep her balance and win the battle of survival.

Suddenly, Gavin was at her side and with strong grips, clamped on to her arm with one hand, while tightly grasping on to the chain with the other hand . . . Then it was all over. . . She was still standing. The wave reluctantly returned to the sea, empty handed. She (and Gavin) had won.

Shakily, she continued the last few yards with Gavin firmly hanging on to her, and finally had reached the end of the walkway.

"Thank God," she murmured.

"You had me scared there for a moment, Ma'am," said Gavin.

"Yeah, it was a little rougher than I'd anticipated."

She rolled down her pants legs. Rolling them up had been an absolute waste of time and effort. She was completely soaked.

"I'm Gavin Roche, Landlord of the Tides Inn. You do look a little shook up."

"Oh no, I'm okay. Thanks to you, Mr. Roche. I owe you big time."

She certainly didn't want to show any weakness at this point. She was hoping that Roche would blame her shaking knees on the cold, and not that she was actually half scared out of her mind.

They continued moving toward the pub.

Thompkins stated, "Okay, first off, I would like to talk to everyone together. It is safe to assume that everyone is still here, isn't it?"

"Oh yeah. Bunny Chase and Carole Coxton are upstairs. We persuaded Bunny to leave the body and go upstairs. Carole is staying with her."

The two women were just coming down the stairs as Gavin and Thompkins entered the room. . . Bunny was carrying Mimi in her arms.

"Let's pull some chairs around the fireplace for right now, "said Gavin, "Constable Thompkins is pretty well soaked."

"You look a little wet yourself, Gavin," said Brindley.

"Yes," interrupted Thompkins, "I'm sure that if Mr. Roche was still dry, that I would not be here. As I told him, I owe him big time."

"I think I will go upstairs and change some clothes. Constable, would you like something to drink?" asked Gavin.

"No thanks, not while on duty. I could really use a cuppa, though, if you have one."

"Carole, could you go over to the back bar and get the Constable some tea while I go upstairs and change clothes and grab some towels and blankets?" asked Gavin.

Chairs were pulled in front of the fire in a semi-circle facing the fireplace, with Thompkins's chair in the middle facing the group, her back absorbing the warming flames.

Gavin returned down the stairs wearing dry clothes and carrying towels and blankets, just as Carole arrived with the tea.

Thompkins toweled off her long blonde hair and wrapped the blankets tightly around her.

"Thank you, Mr. Roche. The tea especially hits the spot. Our power at the office has been off and I have been dying for one for several hours now."

Ian leaned over and whispered to Derek, "Tea! How did we g't a 'Miss Prissy' for th's job?"

Derek just shrugged.

While still holding a blanket snug to her body, Constable Thompkins got up and walked over to where the body was lying and lifted the covering tablecloth. She took several minutes looking around from several different angles. She then replaced the tablecloth, returned to her chair, positioned the blankets, and sat down.

"Where's Reggie?" asked Carole. "It seems to me that he's the one qualified to conduct this investigation."

"I'm sure he will be along before the investigation is over, but he is off duty right now, and it is my investigation." She immediately regretted the emphatic manner that she had said this. She was sure that her insecurity had seeped through.

Carole diplomatically replied, "Oh no, I'm not questioning your professional competence, but Reggie is a regular here. This is his pub. In fact, he tends the bar for Gavin on occasions, so he knows all that goes on."

"If it is any comfort, I'm sure he will be in charge when he is again available. Now, can we get on with it? I have a few questions to ask."

During the questioning Thompkins determined that everybody but the victim was at the bar or in the dart area. The victim came up to get a refill in the glass that he had been using. He had complained that the last time Roche had not given him the proper ale. Several people watched the pouring of the beer. If poison was the cause of the death, it appears that it almost impossible to have added it at that point. Chase returned to his chair. A short time later, while the goal replay was being shown, Chase left his chair and went to the WC. Even though everyone was engrossed in the replay at the bar and not paying any attention to Giles' corner while he was gone, it was virtually impossible for anyone to cross through the dart area, through a row of tables, add the poison, and return to the bar without being noticed. It would have been too risky.

The table that the victim was sitting at was basically his when he was at the pub. If someone was occupying it when Giles came in, he made it clear that it was his, which all the regulars knew.

Suddenly a voice boomed from the entrance. "What the hell is going on here!"

The figure of a tough hard-boiled man, with slicked back dark hair filled the doorway.

"Hello, Reggie," said Gavin. "Boy are we glad to see you. We have had a little trouble here. It seems like someone finally got their fill of Giles."

"So. What happened?"

"Someone slipped him a little poison."

"What! Giles. Is he dead?"

"He's dead."

A scowling Reggie Duke then turned to Thompkins, "Why didn't you call me?"

"You said that you weren't feeling well. And when you left to go home, you did say that you did not want to be disturbed under any circumstances. Besides, I've got it under control."

"I just bet you have it under control! I'll take over now, Constable. Gavin, draw me a pint."

Ian again leaned over to Derek and whispered, "At least, we finally g't a real man on the job now."

Duke looked over at Thompkins and grinned, "Constable, you look like a drowned hen."

Thompkins glared back.

Duke continued, "Has the lab been informed?"

"Yes, the lab people and the paramedics have been notified and will be here any minute now," answered Thompkins.

Duke walked over and examined the crime scene, then returned to the bar area where he was filled in on all the details, most of which was a repeat from the information provided to Thompkins

The lab crew arrived and immediately descended on the scene, dusting Giles's glass and the area for fingerprints. They also fingerprinted everyone at the scene. After an hour they had completed their investigation.

As he was leaving, the lab crew chief went over to Duke, "Don't think there's any question about it, it was poison. I'll have the lab check the glass, but I also don't think there's any doubt about it being the poison source. I'll have the body removed."

Duke announced to those remaining, "Well, I guess that about wraps it up. Everyone can leave if you want to. Constable, I'll meet you in the office tomorrow, say noon."

Thompkins glowered, "Okay, Chief. . . However, I was offered a drink when I arrived, and since I'm off duty now and my clothes are almost dry, I think I will take you up on that offer, Mr. Roche."

"With pleasure, Constable. Do you want another, Reggie?

"I'm ready."

Bunny and Carole moved across to the far corner of the room. The rest returned to the bar, while Gavin poured more pints.

Thompkins was standing next to Ali Ahmed when her beer arrived. The two started discussing Egypt and the antiquities, and his pharmaceutical business, which Ali made clear were legitimate drugs. The rest of the crew discussed the football match.

"Reggie, did you see the end of the match," asked Derek.

"You mean did I see that fluky kick. You bet I did."

"That was na fluky kick. Barstone just guided it in," said Ian.

"While lying flat on his back! The damn thing hit his foot by accident. He had no idea where the ball was, or where it was going, for that matter." said Duke.

"You g't to be kidding. He stretched out and kicked it dead on with his foot. It didn't just hit and ricochet. Th't was a great eff'rt," said Ian.

"It was just plain luck," said Derek.

"It w's skill," said Ian.

"It was luck."

While talking to Ali, Thompson was watching and listening to the banter at the bar. She looked over to the corner where Bunny was staring straight ahead. Carole was sitting next to her, talking to her and holding her hand. Sadness engulfed Thompkins's face.

At the same time Dr. Brindley, leaning against the bar, drink in hand, looked around. He pursed his lips. Then under his breath he murmured, "Hard to believe. One of these people is a murderer . . . People that I know so well. So well for so long. Or thought I knew. So much for camaraderie."

Chapter Four
The Doctor Is Here

Thompkins arrived at the station a little past noon the next day. Duke was waiting and motioned her to a chair in front of his desk.

"Sit down. How is your part of the investigation going?"

"I've spent the morning doing a lot of checking around. Been to the bank. Talked to quite a few people. One thing about this town, the folks love to gossip.

'Okay, so you've been earning your pay. What have you found out?"

Just then Dr. Brindley walked in.

Duke said to Thompkins, "I want to know everything you found out. But I asked Dr. Brindley to drop by, and here he is. I'll catch up on your findings after he goes."

Duke looked at Brindley and motioned to a chair, "Good afternoon, Hamish. Sit down."

Brindley pulled up a chair and sat next to Thompkins. Duke said, "Hamish, we are going to be questioning everyone who was there at the time Giles was poisoned. Not that we suspect you, but maybe you can give us some help with what you saw."

"I understand, but I'm afraid I can't give you much help."

Thompkins jumped in, "Obviously I guess our first question is, did you see anything suspicious?"

Duke glowered at her, then added, "Yes, Hamish. Anything suspicious?"

"No. The dart players seemed to be absorbed in their game or the football match. I did not see anyone going close to Giles."

Duke asked, "And what about when Arsenal scored?"

"Everyone went over to the telly."

"Are you sure, everyone?" asked Thompkins.

Duke glared at Thompkins again.

Thompkins then continued, "And are you sure they all stayed there?"

"I am positive. No, no one left the telly."

"So you are sure you have no idea how the poison could have been injected in his beer?" asked Duke.

"No, I sure don't."

"Do you have any idea of anyone who had a reason to kill Mr. Chase?" questioned Thompkins.

Duke's disgusted look returned to his face, then added, "Constable, many people didn't like the ole bugger."

Brindley answered anyway, "Yes, a lot of people didn't like the guy, especially anyone who had business dealings with him. But I can't think of anybody that hated him that badly."

"Dr. Brindley did you have any business dealing with Mr. Chase at all?" asked Thompkins.

"None at all. I don't do much in the way of dealing in business. . . With anyone."

Thompkins continued, "Was the victim a patient of yours?"

Duke interrupted, "Constable. Everyone in this village was Hamish's patient. That was a stupid question."

Brindley answered anyway, "Yes, Giles was one of my patients. Had been for as long as I have been practicing here, which is many years."

"Did he have any health problems lately?"

"No. Nothing serious."

"Nothing that could be connected with this case?"

Brindley shook his head. "No. Nothing I can connect it to."

There was a lull.

Duke then said half sarcastically, 'Well, Constable, do you have any other questions? Any that make sense. It doesn't sound like it."

Thompkins looked away, "No, not at the moment."

"Okay. I don't have any more questions either. So, I guess we can wrap this one up."

"That was quick and easy," said Brindley

Duke then switched subjects, "That was quite a football match yesterday. Arsenal is tough."

Arsenal is always tough. They have really rewarded us supporters. And we have stuck with them through thick and thin."

"Yeah, all except Giles. I wonder what made him drop them?"

"Oh, I think he just decided to drop all of football. Well, I got things to do."

Both Duke and Brindley stood up and walked to the front door. At the door, Duke shook Brindley's hand.

Brindley looked over Duke's shoulder, "Goodbye Constable.

Thompkins stood up. "Goodbye Dr. Brindley".

Thompkins walked back to her desk and sat down.

Brindley exited.

Duke walked back to where Thompkins was seated, purposely towered over her, and intimidatedly looked down at her. "Constable let's not forget that I," pointing to his chest, "am responsible for the questioning".

Duke quickly turned and also headed to the door. As he left, he said, "I got things to check on. I'll be back in an hour or so. We can check on Bunny then."

Chapter Five
Bunny's House

Duke and Thompkins drove the four miles, most of which was through wooded terrain, to Bunny's house. The house was luxurious, could almost be called a mansion.

While on the way, Thompkins shared, "In my investigations, I found that several people believed that Bunny Chase and Ian O'Brien . . ."

"Were having an affair." Duke interrupted. "That's not earthshaking. Everyone at the pub knew that. I think even Giles knew. Feel free to ask her about it."

Thompkins just looked at him and shook her head.

They knocked on the front door.

A maid, Jessie dressed in typical maid attire answered.

"Good morning, Jessie", greeted Duke.

"Good morning, Sergeant."

"Is Mrs. Chase in?"

"She is around in the back."

"Constable Thompkins and I would like to see her."

"I will take you back."

Jessie led Duke and Thompkins around the side of the house to the back patio. The spacious, well-landscaped backyard was every bit as luxurious as the house itself. Lush green grass spilled over and filled in between many beautiful shrubs and trees.

Bunny was seated at a patio table drinking tea, with Mimi in her lap.

"Good morning, Bunny," said Duke.

Thompkins added her greeting.

"Good morning, Reggie...Constable. Would you like some tea?"

"Thank you, that would be nice." said Thompkins

"Yeah, I'll take some." added Duke.

Bunny, to the maid "Jessie, please bring some cups and more biscuits."

"Mrs. Chase, you have a lovely place here. The grounds are so beautiful." commented Thompkins.

"Thank you, Constable. Giles and I spent many wonderful times here. It is very peaceful."

"And you have thrown some great parties," added Duke.

"Yeah, we have had a few, haven't we Reggie?"

Thompkins expressed her sympathy, "I am really sorry. We hate to intrude at this time."

"Yes, Bunny. I'm very sorry too. But we do have to ask you a few questions. Are you up to it?" asked Duke.

"Yes. I think so."

"We are hoping that you can give us some help with our investigation." said Thompkins.

"I will try."

Duke led off, "Did you see or hear anything that felt out of the ordinary?"

"No. I was either playing darts or watching the football match most of the time."

Duke asked, "Anything strange with any of the others?"

"No. We were all together, all of the time. There is no way anyone had any chance to do anything."

Jessie returned with two cups and biscuits. There is a pause in the conversation as Jessie placed the cups in front of Duke and Thompkins, and the biscuits in the middle of the table. She then turned and left. Bunny poured.

All of a sudden Mimi jumped off Bunny's lap and strolled around the area and out on the grassy area.

"You will have to excuse Mimi, I think she had to go." explained Bunny.

Immediately Mimi returned, was lifted up to Bunny's lap and settled in again.

Tompkins continued, "Did Mr. Chase have any enemies?"

"Oh, he had a few conflicts in his business. But I don't know of any that were serious enough to kill him."

"I don't think I know. What was his business?" asked Thompkins.

Duke answered Bunny, "He was in the Import/Export business. 'Chase Import and Export'."

"I see. Is there any chance that there were any shady parts of the operation?"

With anger in her voice, Bunny answered, "NOT WITH GILES! He was a very honest man. I can vouch that everything he did was conducted in a very honorable way. He may have had a very grouchy manner. And some people didn't like him because of that. But that was no reason to kill him, was it?"

Thompkins then said to Bunny, "In my investigations, I found that several people believe you and Ian O'Brien were having an affair."

Bunny stared at her. "What kind of accusation is that? Ian and I are just friends. Nothing else. Nothing. I don't think that is a proper question."

After a short pause, Duke changes the subject, trying to defuse the situation. "Bunny, I understand that you and Giles had a prenuptial agreement." added Duke.

"That is correct. It was at my insistence. I wanted to remove any doubts that I loved him, not his money."

Tears started flowing from Bunny's eyes. She took a napkin from the table and wiped her eyes. She sniffled.

Looking concerned, Duke said, "Constable, I think maybe under the circumstances we should wait until another day."

This concern surprised Thompkins. Then she said, "Yes, Sergeant, I agree."

Duke stood up. "Thank you for your time, Bunny".

Thompkins stood up. "And again, I am very sorry about your loss."

"Thank you, Constable."

"Don't get up." said Duke.

"Goodbye, Reggie. . .Constable"

Duke and Thompkins walked through the lawn area, toward their car. Bunny, while stroking Mimi, watched them as they left.

As they went around the corner of the house and out of sight of Bunny, Thompkins said "Well Bunny certainly tried to give the impression that she was a loyal, devoted wife."

"That she did . . . I also was surprised at her claim about the prenuptial agreement being her idea. But it means theoretically, with the agreement, that Bunny won't get a large amount of his money. That eliminates that motive for Bunny."

"Maybe. Maybe not. In talking to his solicitor this morning, I found out that Mr. Chase had updated his will. The revision contradicted the agreement."

"That's interesting. Why would he do that?"

"I wonder if she knew about the will change?"

Thompkins said, "Maybe under the circumstances we should not have asked her about the affair."

"Maybe. But it is no surprise that she denied it."

"Getting back to this will, maybe he really did love her. Maybe enough to trust her." said Thompkins.

Duke nodded his head, "Maybe so."

Duke and Thompkins then drove off.

"While we are out, let's drop by Derek Finnegan's shop," said Duke.

Chapter Six
Gadgets, Gadgets, Gadgets

Duke and Thompkins drove into the center business section of Hopkins Bay to Finnegan Enterprises, a small shop building off of a small side street, with only a small wooden sign in the window: -FINNEGAN ENTERPRISES-.

Duke and Thompkins exited the car parked in front of the shop and proceeded to the front door. Thompkins stopped at the door and said to Duke, "Before we talk to Mr. Finnegan, I must tell you of some information that I found out this morning."

"What is that?"

"Chase was backing one of Finnegan's inventions, one that is possibly going to be a big moneymaker. Finnegan is a great inventor but a lousy businessman. Somehow, Chase and his solicitors set up the agreement so that Chase got the gravy and Finnegan got peanuts."

"That is interesting. Hummm. I had heard some rumors to that effect. That could certainly be a motive."

Duke turned and entered the shop with Thompkins following. Derek Finnegan was seated at a desk to the side of the room. The room was cluttered. There were three long tables set up. One was covered with all kinds of objects: plastic tubing, electrical and electronic wire, electronic boxes, rags, switches, tools, and etc. on them. A series of wires were spread out spider-like from a small plastic box to a series of switches, to more various sized boxes. One of the wires was a thick electrical wire plugged in to an electrical plug in the wall.

Thompkins walked over and looked at it from several angles.

A second long table was loaded with tools of various kinds with a drone in the middle.

Derek stood up. "Good afternoon Reggie . . . Constable. What brings you here?"

Reggie nodded.

Thompkins scanned the tabletop, "Good afternoon, Mr. Finnegan."

Duke said, "We just stopped in to see if you have any information that would help us with our investigation."

Thompkins continued looking around the rest of the room. "My goodness, this is quite impressive".

Duke turned and also looked around the room. "Impressive? Looks like a bunch of junk to me."

"I don't see junk, I see a lot of imagination".

"Well thank you, Constable. You know I think I like imagination better than junk," answered Derek.

Thompkins then walked over to the third table with a large assortment of gadgets gathered together. "My goodness, what is going on here?"

"Just a little project for one of my international clients, you know".

"Who?" asked Duke.

Derek responded, "Afraid I can't answer that. One of the main aspects of my agreement is confidentiality, you know what I mean.

"That sounds somewhat sinister, if you know what I mean," responded Duke, "Is it a, local company?"

"No. A U.K. company was in competition at one time, but I ended up with a foreign company."

All three returned to Derek's desk area and sat down.

Thompkins asked, "And you were the one that invented and setup the system for Ole' Pete's tide alarm at the Tides Inn, weren't you?".

"That is my jewel. I had my doubts going in, but it seems to be working quite well, you know what I mean."

"I have to admit that it is an amazing system." said Thompkins. "And I love the diver action. So clever."

"Thank you. Would both of you like some tea?"

"Don't think so. We won't be long," answered Duke. "Now what can you tell us about the other night?"

"I don't think I can tell you anything of help. I was playing darts with Ian, Bunny and Carole. We were all together the whole time leading up to when Giles keeled over. None of us could have done anything without the others noticing. It just seems impossible."

"In my investigations," said Thompkins, "I have discovered an interesting fact. Mr. Chase was backing one of your inventions, one that looks like it could be a big moneymaker. Now it appears that you are a great inventor, Mr. Finnegan, but a lousy businessman. Somehow, Chase and his solicitors set up the agreement so that he got the gravy and you have ended up with peanuts."

Derek processed the accusation. "Yeah, That's the situation in a nutshell."

"That must result in a lot of anger." said Duke.

"You mean enough to kill Giles. No, you're wrong there, Reggie. Yes, I would have liked to have killed him. But I could never do anything like that. In fact, I think you have to agree, there was really no way I could have, is there?"

"Maybe, maybe not." said Duke.

"However, one thing you should know." Derek pointed to the table with the drone. "Giles and I were partners on that baby. He negotiated the deal. And in addition to his negotiations, the whole deal is dependent on his export license. It also can be a big money maker. But I have a little problem right now, with him dead, don't you know?"

Duke nodded his head. "Yes, I guess you do."

"So, why would I kill him?"

Duke walked over to the drone table and picked up a part and held it up in front of him and looked at it. "Anything else?"

"No," answered Thompkins.

"Well, I guess that's about it. Constable, I guess we better get going."

Thompkins pointed at the collection of gadgets. "Mr. Finnegan, something just came into my mind. That U.K. company that lost out in the project over there, was Mr. Chase a part of that company?"

"Can't say."

"Can't say, or won't say? I should warn you that we can get access to all this information by legal means if we have to."

"Okay. Please keep it confidential. Yes, Giles was the major U.K. person involved.   And not happy about the outcome.   It has the possibilities of being a gigantic money maker, and he was planning to make a big stink about it."

"Law-suit?" asked Duke.

"That and he said he had a few retaliations up his sleeve."

"This must have made the company you went with very nervous."

"Maybe.   But they are pretty high-powered, and I have found can be pretty ruthless. I am a little nervous that I went with them now.

Thompkins stood up. "This is very interesting, Mr. Finnegan. We might need some more information on the parties involved in this."

Duke stood up, and both walked toward the door.

Thompkins continued, "Mr. Finnegan, thank you for your time." Looking around she added, "I am totally impressed by your work here.   You have an incredible imagination".

"I hope so.   That is what I depend on to make my living, don't I".

Duke and Thompkins walked to the door and exited toward their car.

Duke said to Thompkins, "And maybe that imagination was put to use in another way . . . To plot a way to kill Giles."

"I guess that is possible".

"And that information about a conflict between competitors sounds interesting.   I wonder how far the winning company might go to protect their interests?"

"To kill for it?"

Duke shook his head. "And by the way, what was that *'I should warn you that we can get access by legal means if we have to'*. Where did that come from?"

"Hey, it worked."

Duke kept shaking his head.

Chapter Seven
From Foreign Lands

At the Hopkins Bay Police Station the next day, Duke and Thompkins were seated at their desks when Ali Ahmed entered.

"Oh, Mr. Ahmed, do come in. Constable bring two chairs over."

As Thompkins started to drag the chairs over, Ali moved over and took hold of them. . . "Here let me help you with these."

After Ali had the chairs in place, and he and Thompkins were seated, Duke said, "Mr. Ahmed, thank you for coming in. We would like to ask you a few questions. We certainly hope that you can give us some help with our investigation. Would you like any coffee or anything.?"

Ali declined the offer.

"I guess our first question then, for the record, is what is your business in Hopkins Bay?" asked Duke.

"As I said before, I am a pharmaceutical salesman selling drugs."

"Where is your home?" chimed in Thompkins.

"I live in Cairo, Egypt. We have a very thriving pharmaceutical industry there."

Thompkins said, "I have visited Cairo. Several times. A very interesting and exotic country."

"We do have our share of interesting and historical sites."

"Do you have family there?"

Ali pulled out his cell phone and pulled up a photo and showed it to Thompkins.

"You have a good-looking family," said Thompkins

"Thank you."

Duke shook his head in disgust. "What passports do you own?"

"I actually have dual citizenship, Egyptian and British."

"Why two?" asked Thompkins.

"My father worked in the U.K. for 12 years. He was director in charge of the Egyptian Antiquity Exhibit at the British Museum in London. I was born here in the U.K."

With admiration Thompkins said, "Antiquities . . . At the Museum. I love that place. It is my favorite place to explore."

"I was born shortly after my parents moved here. So fortunately, I satisfied the 'born here', and the '10 year residency' requirements for citizenship."

"But you live in Egypt now." said Duke.

"Yes."

"You're involved in antiquities now?" asked Thompkins.

"You might say so, but not directly. My father is now the Egyptian Minister of Antiquities. I have an obvious strong, related interest. I too love antiquities."

"But you don't have any official tie to them?"

"None what-so-ever."

"I notice at Tides Inn you had no aversion to alcohol." said Thompkins.

"None what-so-ever. My English side is in control of that segment of my life."

Thompkins and Duke chuckled.

Duke inquired, "I think our biggest interest at this time is why you are spending time in a little out of the way place like Hopkins Bay?"

"Yorkshire is one of my best areas in England. This area has always been very good to me. I usually stay in Hull or York, but in driving around the area I have always been intrigued by Hopkins Bay. So, I decided on this trip to make it my base."

Duke then asked, "Have you been to the Tides Inn before?"

"Not really. I have driven by several times and I planned to stop, but it seems like each time the water was over the walkway and I was unable to get in. So, timing it right was part of my plans this time."

"Did you know, or have you ever met any of the people that were at the pub the other night, the night of the murder?" queried Duke.

"No. No one."

Thompkins asked, "Do you have anything that you would like to add to the investigation? Anything?"

"No. No, no I really don't."

"Constable? Anything else?"

"Nope."

"O.K., I guess we are finished," concluded Duke.

"Mr. Ahmed," said Tompkins, "As I indicated before, I have a real strong love of Egypt and its antiquities. I would certainly like to talk to you more about one of my favorite subjects."

"It would be my pleasure, Ma'am. Maybe on your next trip to Egypt."

Duke said impatiently, "You are free to go."

As Ali reached the door, Thompkins said, "Thank you for coming in, Mr. Ahmed. How long before you see your family?"

"Another week, 'Inshallah', God willing."

"I know they will be glad to see you."

"Not as glad as I will be."

Ali opened the door and exited.

"So, what do you think Constable?"

"Well on the surface, he looks like an innocent salesman. Family man, etc. I liked him." Then after a pause Thompkins added, "But I don't know, it could be fertile grounds for a lucrative smuggling operation. . . . drugs and/or antiquities; UK and Egypt; exports and imports. All that combined has all the makings of something sinister.

"Yeah, very sinister."

Chapter Eight
Care-For-You

The 'Care-For-You-Chemists' business was owned by Carole Coxton. It was in a modest, non-descript shop with:
-- CARE-FOR-YOU-CHEMISTS –
painted on the wall above a wide front window. Duke and Thompkins parked their car in front and walked to the front door.

"One thing you should know before we talk to Carole Coxton." said Duke. "Giles and Carole were once an item. But then Giles dumped her for a younger, much more attractive Bunny. Carole has been bitter ever since."

"A woman scorned, huh. That has the makings of a very bitter woman."

"There's also a rumor, and I emphasize, rumor, that in a romantic moment Carole confided in Giles about a prescription mistake she had made that caused grave problems to one of her customers. The rumor is that Giles has been blackmailing her ever since."

"That is interesting."

"This is a rumor, I again emphasize, but another intriguing piece to puzzle."

"Hum," murmured Thompkins.

"Feel free to ask her about it."

Thompkins looked at Duke, shook her head and smiled.

The interior was a typical Chemist Shop, several rows of aisles with shelves loaded with different bottles and small boxes.

Carole, dressed in chemist attire, happened to be on the floor just finishing with a customer. The customer continued to the counter where a lady, also in chemist attire, waited to check her out.

Carole looked up, "Hello Reggie."

"Hello Carole. How are you?"

"I'm fine."

"Constable Thompkins and I would like to ask you a few questions about the incident at the Tides".

"Of course. Hello Constable."

Thompkins nodded.

"Let's go into my office."

Carole leads the way to a door at the rear of the shop. They enter. Carole sits down behind a desk, Duke and Thompkins sit on a sofa opposite.

Duke asked, "Did you see or hear anything that could help us with our investigation?"

"No. I really am sorry. I didn't see anything out of the ordinary."

"Did you leave the dart area at any time?"

"Sure. We all went over to our table between games and got our drinks refreshed and watched some of the football match."

"Did any of the others in your group leave for any length of time or do anything that seemed out of place?"

"No. I am sure that we were all together all of the time. I don't think anyone had any chance to do anything. How could they?"

"It is my understanding," continued Thompkins, "that you and Mr. Chase had a romantic attachment at one time."

Carole looked at Duke. Duke turned his head slightly away, the corners of his lips creeping upward into a smile.

Carole hesitated, "Romantic Attachment?", another slight delay. "Yeah, I guess you could call it that . . . We were pretty close . . . I guess."

"Close enough to share secrets?" asked Thompkins.

Carole stared at the floor . . . "That . . . That is a very personal question, Constable."

Thompkins and Duke said nothing, just kept looking at Carole. Several moments of silence followed. Finally, Carole in a low voice, "No".

More silence as Thompkins and Duke waited for further comment, but none was forthcoming.

Finally, Duke broke the silence, "There were rumors, Carole, about a prescription error."

Indignantly Carole answered, "Rumors. They must have been wrong, weren't they? I admit we had a fling. But WE DID NOT EXCHANGE SECRETS - OF WHICH I HAVE NONE".

Another long pause.

Thompkins then asked, "Do you have any idea who would have poisoned Giles? Do you know anyone who had a reason?"

"No, I don't. Now if you don't mind, I have some prescriptions that need to be prepared".

Duke and Thompkins both stood up.

Thompkins said, "Thank you, Mrs. Coxton".

"I'm sorry, Carole", said Duke. "It can get a little awkward in situations like this."

Carole answered very briskly, "Yes, It can, can't it."

Duke and Tompkins exited and walked toward their car.

"Well, she certainly didn't tell us anything more than we already knew." said Thompkins.

"Doesn't look like it." Then grinning at Thompkins "But she did get pretty feisty about her relations with Giles. Well, while we are out, let's drop by and see Ian O'Brien."

Chapter Nine
Ship Ahoy

The Hopkins Bay Marina was a short distance out of town on the highway that runs along the coast.

On the way to see Ian O'Brien informed Duke, "I do have some information about Mr. Thompkins O'Brien that I discovered in my research. Mr. O'Brien was a member of the IRA several years ago."

"What! I never heard that before. Where did you get that information?"

"I requested information on Mr. O'Brien from our record department. He spent some time in prison."

"What for?"

"Don't know. That is about all I know right now. I just found out. Guess we can ask him."

Just then the turnoff to the left to Hopkins Bay Marina came up. The office came up shortly after on the left and faced five rows of docks, lined with boats of various sizes, shapes and usage, including recreation boats, sailboats, fishing boats, racing boats.

They parked and got out of the car and walked toward the office.

"So, this is where Ian O'Brien works, huh." said Thompkins.

"Yes. He's the manager. If you ever want to store a boat, this is the place. In fact, it is about the only place, unless you have a private dock at your house. Or you can rent one."

"I'll keep that in mind."

"It is also the place to buy a boat."

"I don't have any desire to own a boat, but it I ever get one, I will remember that."

Duke chuckled.

When they entered the office, Ian, seated at his desk greeted them. "How ya' Reggie. . . . Constable."

Duke answered. "Good morning, Ian."

Thompkins answered, "Good morning Mr. O'Brien "And then added, "You certainly have some nice looking boats out there."

"Ya I do. Want to buy one. I have quite a few."

"Not today, I'm afraid."

"Ta bad. I g't some great deals."

Duke then added, "Ian, we have a few questions for you, if you have the time."

"In regard 'ta' Giles demise?"

"That's right. Did you see or hear anything that felt like it was out of the ordinary?"

"Nah, I don' think so. I was playin' darts most of the time."

"Did any of the others leave for any length of time or did anything seem out of place?" asked Thompkins.

"Nah. I am sure that we were all tagetder all de time. I cant think of a time when anyone had any chance to do anything."

"Did Mr. Chase have any enemies that you knew of?"

"I guess it's possible. But I don't t'ink so."

"Do the four of you play darts often?" asked Thompkins.

"We git tagetder probably two or three tim's a week."

"Is it always the four of you?"

"Most of the tim'e."

"And if one of you can't make it?"

"On an odd occasion we be jo'ned by someone else. Hamish jo'ns sometimes. Som'times it's som'one else. But usually we dont play if one of us is tied up."

"Did Chase ever play?"

"Some time ago he did. In fact when we initially got started, he was a regular and played most ah da tim'e. But he just seemed to lose intrst."

Duke added, "I haven't seen him playing in a long time."

Thompkins continued the questioning. "And what is your relationship with Mrs. Chase?"

Ian took some time to digest this question. Then with anger in his voice answered." I dont have, nor have I ever had any relationship wid Mrs. Chase! None! Zero! Not on yer Nelly."

The room was quiet for a few moments.

Thompkins finally broke the silence. "I'm sorry, Mr. O'Brien. But in an investigation like this, pointed questions have to be asked."

Duke then brought up the question of the IRA membership. "Ian, during our investigation a little matter of your IRA involvement has surfaced."

Ian pursed his lips. After a delay he finally answered, "I was afra'd that was goin' to come up. Yes, I was involved with IRA somewhat. It was a lon' time ago, when I was a yo'ng idealist. I didn't da anything really drastic. But there was un IRA rally and I felt my obligation to ga to it. I thought it was goin' to be just a peaceful, noisy rally. But it turn'd violent. And I w's arrested. And I spent two years in the goal. When I g't out there was a strong movement to get me back in the fold. But by then I didnt want any part of it. I vowed to ne'er have anything ta do with the IRA again, and I ha'vn't And I ended up here."

"That is quite a story," commented Duke. "I wonder why this information has not surfaced before now?"

"It h's nothin' to do with Giles' murder, I promise ya."

"Yes, I don't see any connection either. But we will still keep it under consideration."

"Nobody around her' knows about this right now. Does it have ta come out?"

"We'll see. Depending how the investigation goes."

The room remains silent for several moments.

"Constable, have you any further questions?"

"No, I don't think so."

Duke stands up. "Okay. I think we have taken up enough of Mr. O'Brien's time."

Thompkins also stands up. "Thank you for your time, Mr. O'Brien."

Ian nods. But does not move. Duke and Thompkins exit the Hopkins Bay Marina office.

Duke said, "Well that I.R.A. was some surprise. Ian has never caused any trouble. I guess there could be some connection to the murder, but it sure escapes me how. I cannot believe that this has never become common knowledge. I'm sure I should have known about this long ago."

"Yes, we have to keep in mind that there could be some connection."

"And, he didn't take that question about he and Bunny's relationship very kindly."

Thompkins nodded.

Chapter Ten
The Tides Inn

After checking the tide schedule, Thompkins arrived at the entrance to the Tides Inn about two o'clock that afternoon and crossed over the pathway to the Inn. Trickles of water from the previous flood covering were still finding their way over the edge from the top surface of the walkway and dripping back to the sea. She found Gavin, wearing an apron, sweeping the pub floor.

"Good afternoon, Mr. Roche, how're you this afternoon?"

"Fine, Constable. Have you found our murderer yet?"

"Not yet, but I'm sure now that the Sergeant is on the case, it will be solved very soon."

"I'm sorry about that, Constable. I think the crew and I were a little rough on you the other night. I'm afraid that it is going to take the people of the town a little while to accept a woman in your job. Especially, if I may be allowed to be frank, a very attractive woman. And the fact that you're new in the village adds a double whammy. But I like your spunk. I think you will do just fine."

"Well thank you for your vote of confidence, Mr. Roche . . . and the compliment."

"You also have to understand that Reggie is a regular here, and the folks are used to him and have a lot of confidence in him. He has done a good job, and the people respect him, so that has made things more difficult for you."

"I understand, Mr. Roche. Also, I do again want to thank you for getting me across the flooded walkway the other night. You might have just saved my life."

"You are very welcome."

Now I wonder if I could look around?"

"Of course, Constable."

Thompkins walked over to where the body had been lying.

"We all know this as 'Giles Corner'", said Roche. "He always sat at this table. He even had a bottle of antacids in the drawer. Had heartburn big time."

Thompkins walked over and opened the drawer.

"There isn't any bottle there now."

"Huh, that is strange."

"Maybe the lab crew took them."

Thompkins then walked to the middle of the room and did a 360 look around. She gazed at the goldfish swimming in the aquarium. Ole' Pete was settled on the bottom.

She then looked at Gavin, "How many rooms do you rent out?"

"Four altogether."

"Are they all occupied?"

"Just one, the one that Mr. Ahmed is in. We did use one temporarily when we took Bunny up to rest and get away from the sight of her husband lying there."

"Are they all locked?"

"No. I don't lock many doors around here. Not much reason to."

"Do you mind if I go up and look at them."

"Not at all. Here, why don't I give you the key for Mr. Ahmed's room, number four, just in case he did lock his door. You can take your time and look around."

"Thanks. Which one did you use for Mrs. Chase?"

"Number two."

"And I assume you live on the premises."

"Yes, I have a small living quarter area upstairs also. If you turn right at the top of the stairs, it is the door at the end of the hall. Look around if you want. You will find that I'm not the best at neatness."

"I assume it's not locked either."

Gavin nodded.

Thompkins walked up the stairs and checked each room closely. She delayed a while in Ahmed's room. His luggage was stashed in the closet, as were his hanging clothes. There didn't appear to be any of his sales items present. She figured he probably had them with him.

She then proceeded to the room that Bunny Chase used. The room appeared to be completely empty. Only a few well-used tissues in the trashcan and on the floor.

Roche's room at the end of the hall contained a small bedroom, kitchenet, sitting area, and attached bath. She spent several minutes examining the rooms and then returned downstairs, where she handed the key to room number four back to Gavin.

"How did it go?" asked Gavin.

"Fine. Is everyone aware that you don't lock things up?"

"Don't know. Guess so. Never thought about it much."

"Okay, what about downstairs? What is there?"

"There is no downstairs. This place is built on solid rock. A basement is impossible."

"Then what else is there that I haven't seen?"

"The building has some storage rooms that I have added on to the outside. The room behind the bar is the refrigerated cask room. All the ale casks are stored there. The ones in use are tapped, and the beer pumped into the bar."

"What else is there on the outside?"

"Behind the back wall, there're two storage areas, one for food products, and another mostly for cleaning supplies."

"Do you mind if I look around back there?"

"Not at all. I'll give you the tour."

They went through a door behind the bar into the cask room. Rosko followed. Scattered around the floor were about a dozen casks, some hooked up to hoses, some stored full and some empty. Cases of beer and loose bottles of various liquors were stored on several combinations of shelves. Some small tools were hanging from the wall.

"The hoses from the casks. Do they go through the wall to the bar?" asked Thompkins.

"Yep, through chilled lines, straight from cask to pump. It's quite a science to prepare and tap the casks correctly. Cask ale is fragile. It is served from the same barrel in which it was fermented. It is naturally carbonated by still active yeast that remains in the ale, rather than by adding carbon dioxide. Unlike normal draft beer, which can remain fresh for up to a month, once a cask is open it has about a five-day shelf life. It must be cellared and dispensed properly."

"I can see that you take great pride in your ale."

"I want my patrons to think of my ale as not just drinkable, but quaffable."

"Very interesting. I don't suppose an off duty female Constable could get a part time job here?"

"You would always be welcome to help out."

"I just might take you up on that some time."

"Look forward to it."

After looking around more, Thompkins said, "I think I'm through here. If it is okay with you, I would like just to look around the other storerooms and the outside area."

"Help yourself. Do you want the super-duper tour?"

"No thanks. I don't want to tie you up anymore. You're busy with your work. I can handle that."

Thompkins went from the bar through a door into the first storage room. Several shelves were filled with food supplies and extra cooking utensils. A big walk-in refrigerator and freezer were side by side against the side wall. She entered both, examining many of the items. She was then taken back, when coming out of the freezer, she noticed a dead rat in the corner right next to it. "Ugh" she uttered. She prodded with the toe of her shoe, turning its stiff body over on its other side. "Ugh." She again uttered and shook her head.

Then she walked to the other side of the room and in that corner, she noticed a long extension pole with a basket on the end. She picked it up, extended it in and out and studied it for a few minutes before returning it to its resting place. As she returned the extension pole, a skull and cross-bones decorated box on a shelf caught her eye. Yes. This was probably the poison used on the rat. She took it off the shelf and examined the listed contents. A short time later she again exited into the pub area.

"Still doing okay, Constable?"

"Yes, thank you. By the way you have a dead rat in there in the corner."

"Ah ha, I finally got that little critter. That new poison I got finally nailed him. Thanks for letting me know. I will get rid of him immediately."

"I don't think I would call that critter little."

Gavin chuckled.

"By the way," said Thompkins, "could you get me a small container. I need to get a sample of that poison."

"Sure."

Thompkins then entered an obviously added-on room. Rosko followed this time. She looked at the wall facing her, the wall between the storeroom and the bar. It still had the original outdoor siding, and the original outdoor windows. The room was crowded with the usual cleaning supplies, mops, brooms, and other miscellaneous equipment. A counter and cabinet ran along one wall, a closet in one corner, and boxes and papers were piled on top of a chair in the other corner.

She walked around the room and inspected it. She went to a chair in the corner, moved the boxes and papers covering it, and sat down. She looked around. Rosko sat down next to her. Thompkins reached down and petted him.

She picked up a book and then a newspaper and looked through both. She questioned herself, '*I wonder if our little small village crime will ever reach the big time media.*'

After several moments she stood up, and with some indication of being obsessive, tidied up, moved things around, and blew dust off objects. She then returned the boxes and other items to where they were. She then walked to the door, paused, turned back and picked up the newspaper and the book, and placed them in her bag.

She moved to the door at the back wall, opened it, and moved out onto the deck area. The view was magnificent. She walked around the rock patio, examining the area, often stopping to admire the view. No matter where she stood, the views were awesome.

She then proceeded to the front door and entered the pub where she was greeted by Gavin, holding a mop. "Thanks for your time, Mr. Roche. I appreciate it."

"You're welcome. Would you like a cup of tea?"

"Why yes, that would be nice. Actually, I'm afraid that I do have a few questions to ask you."

"Of course. I'll be right back. Make yourself at home at the table over there. By the way, there is a container on the table for your sample."

"Thank you. I'll just take it over to the storeroom and grab the sample."

With that Thompkins went back to the food storeroom, dumped some of the contents of the poison box into the container and returned to the pub and sat down at the indicated table. In the meantime, Gavin had walked around to the back of the bar.

Rosko came over and plopped at Thompkins's feet. She reached down and started petting him.

Gavin commented from behind the bar. "Looks like Rosko has found a friend."

"I love dogs. He must be great company."

"He is one great mutt."

"Have you ever had any problems with him in here?"

"No, he gets along with everyone, dogs and humans a like. . . Except for Reggie's German Shepherds."

"I didn't know he had dogs."

"Yep. Those two are nasty guys. Reggie has learned he can't take them anywhere."

"I'll be darn."

Gavin returned to the table with biscuits and two cups of tea.

As he sat down, Thompkins said "I came across a book on ale in the storeroom that looked interesting. You now have me curious and since I may be working in a pub in the future, I would like to know more about it. I was wondering if I could borrow it?"

"By all means. In fact, keep it with my compliments."

"Well thank you, and an old newspaper. It has a story about my old hometown."

"And where might that be?"

"Scarborough."

"So, you are a Yorkie."

"To my core. But now my Yorkie home is Hopkins Bay."

"Well Hopkins Bay is sure better for it."

"Well, thank you. That makes me feel welcome."

"By the way," said Thompkins, "I see you have an apple-knocker in one of your storerooms. Do you have any apple trees here?"

"Do you mean that extension pole with a basket on the end? Is that what it is called? That was left behind by one of my guests a few months ago. I'm waiting for him to return and retrieve it."

"Oh, I am very familiar with apple-knockers. When I was growing up, we used to go up to a pick-your-own orchard around Wilberfoss and pick apples for us and for all the neighbors. Boy were they good. Especially when right off the tree."

She held her hands up in front of her and imaginatively demonstrated the operation of the apple-knocker. "You expand the pole, to the length that you need, stick the top of the basket around the apple, and jerk it, and the apple just falls into the basket. Much fun."

"So that is how you use that thing. It looks like it might be handy for many things. And I bet it is a great memory of your younger days. Maybe I will try it. I'm sure I can find an apple tree somewhere around here."

There was a pause as Thompkins dials up the memory. Then she said, 'As far as the dead rat. Do think you got it with the box of poison on the shelf in the food storage room?"

"Yeah, I'm sure that it was. You don't think it had any connection with the crime, do you?"

"We'll see. It will need some checking out."

There was a pause, then Gavin changed the subject, "I am just curious, how did you get into Law Enforcement?"

"Law Enforcement? I don't know. It seems like it just happened. I didn't go looking for it. It seems to have just happened. Sort of just found me. But I am glad it did. I enjoy the work."

"Have you run into any obstacles being a woman?"

"Of course. But my father told me that in order to succeed in this man's world, I just had to be better. That has been my creed. But to answer your question, none that I haven't been able to overcome."

"You do seem to have run into a few here in Hopkins Bay."

"To a certain extent. But I am sure it is just temporary. I feel very confident of that."

"You are a very positive young woman. I admire your spirit."

"Thank you Mr. Roche. I do appreciate that."

"You can call me Gavin if you want."

"No. I don't think that is possible as long as there is a murder investigation involved."

"Yes. I understand."

A long pause followed.

Gavin broke the silence, "I assume you are not married."

"Nope. Had a few chances. But none worked out. But I'm not adverse to it. What about you? I assume you aren't either."

"I was . . . once. But then I was also married to the sea. Didn't present itself to a very successful combination."

"Yes, there must have been a big conflict between lifestyles."

"Things got rocky, but I did love her. I decided to give up my life at sea and try to settle down. That was when we bought the Tide. I thought working together would make a difference. Make her happy. At first it did. But it turns out it was just too late. It really wasn't the solution after all. And then, before long she was gone."

"I'm sorry. That is tough. Do you still long for the sea?"

Í do. I get the calling every once in a while. But I think I am now ready to settle down. Anyway, I have the Tide."

"It sounds like you are really attached to it . . . Unfortunately, that brings me to a point where I have to ask you a few questions."

"Fire away."

First off, I want to thank you for allowing me free access to your facilities . . . Now, is there anything that you can think of that could help our inquiries?"

"No. It certainly seems like no one in the pub at that time could have done it. I'm afraid you have quite a challenge on your hands. Someone was sure clever."

"That brings up a pertinent problem. We know that Mr. Chase held the mortgage on the Tide, and that he has threatened to foreclose if you didn't come up with the money soon.".

"Yeah, I did owe him quite a bit."

"He was a regular. Do you really think he would foreclose?"

"I don't know. Old Giles was unpredictable."

"That would have been tough on you. You have obviously put a lot into this place. Love – Money – Time - Labour. This must have made you very angry."

"Yeah. That is very true. But I didn't know if he was really going to foreclose, did I? And I don't believe that you could believe that I would poison somebody based on what I thought they <u>might</u> do?"

"It still gives you a powerful motive."

Gavin looks away, "Not that powerful."

There was an awkward pause. Thompkins then broke it, "Okay, I quess that takes care of my questions for now. By the way, speaking of the 'Tide', I'm curious why you don't just build up the walkway so that there is access at all times?"

Gavin answered with a great deal spirit, glad to change the conversation. "What and ruin the mystique? I don't want to own just any pub. I want it to have its own personality . . . My personality. Also, do you realize how much it would cost to raise the walkway to do any good? A fortune. In fact, the cost from my last venture, to build up the walkway is the main reason that I am so in debt now. . . And, more importantly, I am extremely happy with the way it is now."

"I have to agree. You have succeeded. The Tide does have its own personality. A great personality I must add."

"And because of all this, the place gets plenty of valuable publicity from the uniqueness. We get write ups in beer magazines, travel magazines, and every once in while a celebrity will just pop in. They wouldn't do that if we were just an ordinary pub, now would they?"

"I get your point. But then why don't you have a boat available in case of emergencies, like the other night?"

"Wouldn't do any good. There isn't nothing but a rocky shore around the place. No place that a boat could come ashore, or even get close. The village fathers have been trying to get me to build a dock. But the need for a boat is so rare. So far, I have been able to dodge the bullet.

"I see."

"And anyway, the conditions were too rough the other night for a boat to be out on the water, even if there had been a place to dock. The walkway's expense and damage to the mystique would be tough."

"Well, I certainly hope there aren't any more occurrences. I agree, I like the place just as it is."

"I appreciate that, Constable."

"The cylinder at the back of the room started erupting with Ole' Pete's Sound and Light show."

Both people looked over at it.

Thompkins said, "Guess I had better get going. I have taken enough of your time, and I think I have everything I need for now. Again, thank you very much for your help."

Gavin walked Thompkins as far as the patio where he stopped. Thompkins kept walking to the walkway.

Gavin called out, "Come by for a drink anytime."

Thompkins turned and looked back. "I certainly will."

Gavin kept watching until she reached the end of the walkway and out of sight. A big smile covered his face.

Chapter Eleven
Camaraderie vs. Conflict

That evening Derek, Carole, Brindley and Ali were all standing at the bar. Ian and Bunny, with Mimi in her shoulder bag, were at the end of the bar, standing next to each other. Gavin was behind the bar, Rosko was lying on the hearth, while a few other customers occupied tables along the edge of the bar.

Derek raised his glass of ale in a toast. "Here's to Giles. May he rest in peace."

Everyone at the bar also hoisted their glasses to join in.

Ian added, "Yeah, here's to ye, ye ole' bugger."

But as the glasses were being lifted, Brindley interjected." You all do realize that no one else could have knocked off old Giles except one of us. No one."

All seven looked at each other and quickly lowered their elevated glasses.

"Yeah," added Gavin," That is scary."

After a pause, Carole looked over at Ian and Bunny. "Bunny, I'm surprised to see you here. Shouldn't you be home, grieving?"

Ian answered with anger, "Excuse me!"

"Carole, I don't think that was necessary." cut in Brindley.

"Actually," answered Bunny, "I came here to be with MY FRIENDS'. Home seemed so lonely. I felt this was my place to be. It looks like I was mistaken on MY FRIENDS, wasn't I!"

"Well, Bunny, it certainly appears that you have found one long-standing source of comfort," said Carole.

Ian moved angrily toward Carole. "What'd ye mean, Carole."

"You know what I mean."

Ian got in her face. "Ye got a lot of nerve. Bunny has always been a friend . . . and only a friend. I admit that I felt sorry for her, married to that big bully. But we don't have anything goin'."

Brindley pulled Ian away. Carole chuckled.

Bunny adamantly added, "That's right you old cow."

"Yeah. Sure."

"Besides," continued Ian, "Ye're not so pure yeself. Ye had quite a thing going with Giles a while back until he dumped ye. Lover's revenge?"

Carole stared at Ian as he returned to his place at the bar.

Gavin, trying to defuse the situation said, "Come on everyone. Calm down. Before this happened, we were one big happy family. Where is the camaraderie? Who'se ready for another drink?"

Derek then emphasized, "It still doesn't change the fact that one of us is a murderer, you know."

He pushed his glass over to Gavin where it got refilled and passed back to him.

Ian then passed his glass over to Gavin. "I'm ready too."

Gavin grabbed a clean glass and started pouring the pint. It spurted and sputtered. Foam shot out. "Gotta change the keg. Be right back."

As he exited to the keg room, Derek took a sip of his beer and then followed. As he entered the keg room, Gavin was uncoupling the old keg and preparing the new. Derek quietly stood and observed.

Gavin saw him. "And what are you looking at?"

"I'm just trying to see if there is any way you could have slipped that mickey to Giles."

"What? What are you saying?"

"It just seems like you are the only one who had any opportunity to slip that poison in Giles drink. The only one to actually touch the beer or anything that touched the beer, glass, hose, tap etc. No one else could have. It had to be you. How you did it, I sure don't know. But if you did, I gotta give you credit, it was very clever. Very clever indeed."

"Derek, I didn't have any opportunity. You were there the whole time. In fact, several people, including Giles himself were right there, closeup, watching me pour." Gavin shrugged his shoulder. "So, tell me. How?"

"I sure don't know. But don't get me wrong, none of us will really miss the bastard. We all love this pub and sure wouldn't want to have Ole' Giles ruin it, you know. If he had foreclosed, heaven only knows what he would have done with it."

"By the way, speaking of clever," returned Derek, "you are pretty clever in your own right. Was this the workings of another of your clever inventions? Could you have put together another creative idea? I don't think it is beyond the realm of possibility for you to come up with a creative plan. It has your creativity all over it."

"That is absurd, you know."

"Is it? I'm finished here."

Gavin turned and walked past Derek to the pub area. Derek followed.

Suddenly the cylinder at the back of the room started erupting with Ole' Pete's Sound and Light show.

"O.K.," announced Gavin, "Diver up! Last Call. We will be cut off soon. It is getting late. Time to close down. Ian, do you still want that pint?"

"No. Guess' not. I tin'k it's tim'e to hit the Four Poster Inn."

People started filing out over the walkway. One of the last to leave was Brindley. He stopped and waited just past the patio where the walkway started. Soon Ali joined him.

Gavin went to the front door to lock up and saw the conversation going on and watched for a while.

Ali was saying, "I didn't kill him. Why would I? We three had the perfect setup. You order them, I supply em', and Giles makes the arrangements using his export license. Where can you find a better deal than that?"

"'Made' the arrangements, not "makes" the arrangements."

"Yeah, I guess it is past tense now. But we are going to have to find a new exporter."

"I don't think so. I think I am out as of now."

"Yeah. Since this happened, I am thinking of retiring also. It is getting too risky."

The horn sounded.

"Are you leaving town very soon?"

"No, I have other business to take care of. I 'll be around for a while. Besides, Sergeant Duke told me not to go very far until he gives the go ahead."

The gate started to close.

"I had better get out of here," said Brindley.

The water indicated the onset of the flooding as it started splashing over the walkway. As Brindley moved quickly down the walkway, he looked back over his shoulder.

"Goodbye, Ali. It was good working with you."

"Yes, it was. Masalama, Dr. Brindley."

"See you later."

"Inshallah".

"Yes, God willing."

Seeing Ali returning, Gavin went back to his clean-up. Ali walked past him and started up the stairs to his room.

"I thought you didn't know Hamish when I introduced you when you came." said Gavin as Ali climbed the stairs.

Ali continued up the stairs, "I didn't."

Chapter Twelve
I Did It My Way

Sergeant Duke arrived at the office a little after eleven o'clock the next day.

Thompkins greeted him, "Good morning, Sergeant. How is your investigation going?"

"Not much better than it was yesterday. I'm afraid that this is going to be a tough nut to crack. How about you?"

"Oh, I feel pretty confident we will come up with something fairly soon," said Thompkins cheerfully.

"I wish I was that confident. What do you base that on?"

"Just a feeling right now."

Duke shakes his head in disgust. "It's going to take more than a feeling. Anyway. I think we had better go over the case right now. We don't have an interview with Gavin Roche yet. But let's go on with the others now."

"Okay." Thompkins pulls up a chair in front of Duke.

Duke started, "It looks like we had eight people in the pub. One became the victim. That leaves seven suspects. Let's go over each one starting with the four dart throwers."

"Okay."

Duke began, "Number one suspect is **Bunny Chase**, Wife of the victim. We assume that Bunny Chase and Ian Finch were having an affair. Chase was very rich. Everyone figured she had married Giles for his money. But Giles was very shrewd. He had a Prenuptial Agreement? So theoretically, Bunny wouldn't get a large amount of his money when he died, which would have eliminated a motive for Bunny. And Bunny claims the Prenuptial

Agreement was her idea. And as we know now, Giles had made a will that contradicted the agreement anyway. Which definitely confuses the issue. Why did he do that? So, Constable, what else do you have?"."

"Nothing more on Mrs. Chase. So, we go to Number two. Chase was backing one of **Derek Finnegan**'s inventions, one that is going to be a big moneymaker. Finnegan is a great inventor but a lousy businessman. Somehow, Chase and his solicitors set up the agreement so that Chase gets the gravy and Finnegan peanuts. Question is was that big enough to murder over."

Duke proceeded, "That leaves us with Number three, **Ian O'Brien**. As we covered before, everyone knew he and Bunny were having an affair. With Chase out of the picture, a very lucrative relationship would have opened up for the two of them. And we have that new connection with the IRA. As of now I don't see any connection with that and our case. But it does add another dimension to it."

"He could have learned some devious things during his time with the IRA."

"He very well could have."

And that leaves us with number four," continued Thompkins.

"Yes, **Carole Coxton** said Duke. At one time Giles and Carole Coxton were an item. But then Giles dumped her for a younger, much more attractive Bunny. Carole has been pretty bitter ever since. A jilted lover. Then there is the rumor that in a romantic moment Carole confided in Giles about a prescription mistake she had made that caused grave problems to one of her customers. The rumor is that Giles has been blackmailing her ever since. This is just a rumor I again emphasize, but another intriguing piece to the puzzle."

"That takes care of the dart throwers", said Thompkins "What about Number five, **Dr. Brindley?**"

"What about Dr. Brindley?" responded Duke. "He was there, but we don't seem to have anything that seems to connect him with any wrong-doing.

"Yes, not much reason to suspect him. Agreed. I certainly haven't been able to associate him with anything suspicious either. He seems like the only one that was there that had no motive," Thompkins said.

"Yeah, I don't think there is much of a chance for him to be our murderer."

"Number six. What about that Egyptian?" asked Duke.

"I think the Egyptian has a name, **Ali Ahmed**, I believe."

"Yeah, whatever. Why is an Egyptian trying to sell pharmaceuticals in a little out of the way place like Hopkins Bay? He also has easy access to Egyptian Antiquities."

"So, we are looking at two commodities with a history of illegal dealings, which Mr. Ahmed has access to and could very easily be dealing in. And Mr. Giles is in the import-export business. Interesting combination all the way around, drugs or antiquities or both. Under the circumstances, it could easily be a case of an illicit deal gone bad."

"Yes it certainly could. And finally leaves us with Number seven, **Gavin Roche**." said Tompkins.

"Yes. But we still have to interview him."

"Well actually," said Thompkins. "I dropped by the Tides Inn yesterday afternoon and talked to him."

"What! You did what?" . . . I told you . . . I told you I was in charge. You are not to conduct any interviews alone."

Ignoring Duke, Thompkins continued, "Chase held the mortgage on the Tides Inn. It looks like Mr. Roche has gotten into big debt. Especially his building project to raise the walkway. Due to this, Mr. Chase threatened to foreclose if he didn't come up with the money soon."

"Constable, after what I told you, you still disobeyed my orders."

"I was just following up on the investigation."

"You leave me no choice than to report your insubordination to headquarters."

"Okay. But can we get on with our discussion. What about that foreclosure."

Duke glowered at her, then finally answered, "Yes. I think everyone knew about that, too. We were all worried. Don't know what he would have done with the Tide."

"He was a regular. Would he really have foreclosed?"

"Well, we don't know. He could have foreclosed and sold it. Heaven knows what it would have been turned into. Gavin put a lot of time, money and love into it. Losing the Inn would have been devastating. In fact, we all had a lot to lose. This is our home away from home. Anything else on Gavin?"

"That is about it."

Duke then returned to his desk and sat down. "Well, we seem to have covered all the suspects. Let's take a little time and digest what we have."

"Agreed. We still have a ways to go."

They both go back to studying the papers on their desk.

Then in a demanding voice Duke said, "CONSTABLE, GET ME A CUP OF COFFEE!"

Thompkins' head flew up from her reading, daggers shot from her eyes.

Duke continued staring down at his papers. Then without looking up, he added, "One lump. Not too much cream."

After a few moments, still staring at Duke, she proceeded over to the electric burner on a small sink counter and brewed the coffee as ordered.

As she set the coffee down, she spotted the crime reports on his desk.

"May I see these for a minute?"

Duke pushed the papers over to her. "Help yourself."

Thompkins picked up the reports, took them over to her desk and started studying them. She stopped, stared into space for a few moments, then smiled. Returning the papers to Duke's desk, she picked up his empty cup and pleasantly said, "Sergeant, are you through with this? May I take it?"

Duke looked up with a little puzzlement, thrown off guard by the change in her voice. "Well . . . sure. I'm through."

She started back toward the sink and cleaned up the area. Then gathering up a few items in her handbag, she said, "Okay, I'm going to leave. I've got some things I want to look into. However, I think eventually we will have to ask some more questions. Do you think you can get everyone back at the pub tonight? I think we need to talk to them again."

"Why? "

"Well, we do seem to have a whole lot of questions, but very few answers. Maybe getting them together will provide some missing pieces."

Duke thought for a few moments. "Yeah, maybe so. Might help. I will set it up."

He picked up the tide schedule. After studying the schedule, he said, "How about eight o'clock? We can get in and out okay by then."

"Can you get everyone there?"

"I SAID, I will set it up. But if you're just setting up a big show. . ."

Thompkins ignored Duke. "I've got some more stuff to get together. See you there at eight." ignored Thompkins again.

Duke scowled at her back as she walked out the door. *Dammit, I sure don't need a woman around here trying to make a name for herself.*

Chapter Thirteen
It's All Set Up

"So, do you have everything set up for tonight?" asked Duke who was standing at the bar, gripping a pint of ale.

"Yeah", answered Gavin from behind the bar, toweling off a clean glass. "I have a sign, 'PUB CLOSED FOR PRIVATE PARTY – 8 TO CLOSE' ready to post at the end of the walkway.

"That should do it."

"What is this all about?"

"I just felt that it might be a good idea to get everyone together and see if we can come up with any clue to our murder. We are pretty much dead in the water right now."

"I see. Sounds like you have a good idea there. Well hopefully you can figure it all out. Everyone is pretty edgy right now. We had a little blow up here last night."

"Yeah, I heard."

"How is your new Constable coming along?"

"I can sum it up in one word, 'insubordination.

"Wow. That doesn't sound very good. She seemed pretty sharp when she was here."

"I give her orders and the next thing I know – Bang – She is off doing what I told her not to do . . . I'm getting pretty tired of her."

"But she seems pretty smart."

"Smart! She is dumb as a dodo bird."

"That seems sort of rough. Hasn't she been any help in the investigation?"

"Not at all. In fact, she has been a big hindrance. Getting in the way all the time. I sure don't need her help."

Gavin leaves to get an ale for one of the patrons at the other end of the bar. Duke takes a couple of chugs of his beer, and Gavin returns. "So, what are you going to do about her?"

"I've got an 'Insubordination Report" on my desk right now. I plan on sending it in tomorrow."

"Oh. That sounds pretty drastic. As I said, she really impressed me."

"I don't need a woman around. I don't have one at home, I don't need one at work."

Gavin shakes his head. "Still a report like that seems awfully harsh."

"I have got to get rid of that woman . . . Well got to get going. Got things to do. Got to get ready for tonight."

Duke puts his empty glass down on the bar and heads for the door.

"Yeah, see you tonight," Gavin called after him. "You know, I really think you should reconsider. I think she will surprise you before it is all over."

"Fat chance!" Duke waves his hand as he goes out the door.

Chapter Fourteen
The Truth be Known

It was a little after eight o'clock, and everyone was assembled. It was almost like a social gathering. Everyone was talking and drinking when Thompkins arrived.

"Constable," greeted Duke.

"I see everyone is here. I want to thank you for coming. Especially you, Mr. Ahmed. I understand you delayed leaving."

"Well, the Sergeant is pretty persuasive," said Ali.

Duke grinned.

Thompkins continued, "You might be glad to know that I think I can save us all some time. After compiling all my information this afternoon, I now know who the murderer was and how it was done."

The room echoed with gasps.

"This is just like an old-fashioned movie murder mystery." commented Carole under her breath.

"Yeah, I told you that the textbooks she used for her police work were Agatha Christie novels," said Derek.

"Are you trying to make a big impression, Constable?" asked Duke.

"No, I'm afraid not."

"Okay, then, let's hear what the great crime expert has come up with," said Duke.

"My first thought was that the antacid pills in Mr. Chase's table drawer had something to do with this. Especially, since the pills that were always in that drawer are now missing. We have several pharmaceuticals capable of doctoring them. If the pills were the source of the poison, to throw confusion into the issue, someone could have then added the cyanide to the glass during the time that everyone's attention was diverted to the dying man, to make it appear that ale was the real source of the poison. Once Chase had swallowed the poison pill or pills, they were gone . . . as was all evidence. That would have been a clever plan. And, there is a good chance that they would never have been caught. However, I checked with a couple of pharmaceutical experts, and they stated that in reality, it would have been virtually impossible to inject the poison into an existing tablet. They did say that a new tablet could have been fabricated, but they also pointed out that antacid tablets are chewed, not swallowed, so it would have been almost impossible to hide the taste in the pills. So my enthusiasm for this theory quickly evaporated."

"My enthusiasm for this whole thing is quickly evaporating," uttered Duke. "Constable, will you please get on with it."

"I think Reggie is about to blow," whispered Derek.

"Yeah, I have seen him explode before. It is not pretty," murmured Carole.

"I studied the motives and opportunity of everyone here. But the further I studied, even though some of you have strong motives, the more the opportunity became increasingly impossible."

"Does that mean that none of us here did it?" asked Carol.

"That means it was time to look elsewhere for a solution. The only solution left was that it had to be someone that was hiding outside this room. But then, this also seemed virtually impossible. It would have been very difficult to come out of their hiding place, enter the room, and remain unseen while crossing the room and dropping the poison into the drink."

"Running out of ideas, I decided to come back and visit the pub yesterday afternoon to examine the premises inside and out. The cask room was interesting. I tried to picture someone inducing the poison into one of the hoses between the casks and the bar, perhaps with a needle and syringe. That is possible isn't it Mr. Roche?"

"There are several ways the poison could be introduced in the cask room," confirmed Gavin. "But how would you ever know where it would end up."

"I agree, Mr. Roche. The murderer would have to be sure that the poison ended up poured into Mr. Chase's glass. I don't think that person would risk nailing the wrong person. And there is no evidence that the killer did get the wrong person. So that theory did not seem too creditable."

"She definitely has a flair for the dramatic," whispered Derek to Ian.

"Then I visited the storerooms that are attached to the back of the building. In the food storeroom was a dead, poisoned rat."

Gavin cringed at the thought of what everyone was thinking about a rat in their pub.

Thompkins continued, "The poisoning of Mr. Chase and the rat could have had the same source, a box of commercial pest poison in the room. But I checked the contents listed on the. Box. It did not contain any cyanide. Mr. Roche confirmed that the poison from this box is what he used for the rat. I also took a sample of the poison to the lab, but I haven't received any results yet. But I doubt it contained anything that was not listed. So, it does not appear that this was the poison that killed Mr. Chase."

Moving on to the supply storage room I came across something of interest. There was a stuffed chair in the corner with some boxes and newspapers covering it. I moved the boxes and newspapers and sat down. I was surprised to find that I was staring through a window right into the pub. I could see the whole pub area through the window. I sat there and watched Mr. Roche sweeping and cleaning up for several minutes. I also had a clear view of the telly. There was a curtain on that window, but it was pulled aside. The flowers on Mr.Chase's tabletop, that had been next to Mr. Chase's pint, were there in plain view, just on the other side of the window.

I then picked up the paper off the boxes. Interestingly, it was the Sunday *Telegraph*. . . from the Sunday in question. How is this significant? The Sunday edition doesn't reach Hopkins Bay until sometime in the afternoon. That means someone was in the storage room reading the paper sometime late afternoon, Sunday, the day of the crime. Things were beginning to fall into place."

She cleared her voice. "This is the way I think things transpired. The tide closed the pathway a short time before dark. However, someone carrying the newspaper came across the pathway before the pathway was closed. That person entered the room from the outside, made sure the curtain was closed, and then settled down in the chair with the paper. Just about everyone knew that Roche was lax about locking doors, and the odds were that the door to the storeroom would be left unlocked. Since the sun was still shining there was plenty of light to read the paper. The closet in the far corner offered a safe haven. In the unlikely case that someone were to come into the storeroom, they could duck into the closet out of sight until the visitor left."

"Then darkness fell. The storeroom was dark; the bar was lit. The murderer opened the curtain and settled back down in the chair again, toward the back of the room. The bar area wasn't bright, but there was enough light to aid in making the inside of the storeroom seem dark to anyone looking through the window, at least dark enough to conceal the murderer. The murderer then just sat there patiently passing the time, waiting for the right opportunity to strike."

Thompkins paused for a moment, looking at every face that was now fixed on her. "And hopefully, for the murderer, that opportunity would happen during this tide-in period. If not, there would be other nights. In fact, maybe this wasn't the first attempt. This whole scenario may have taken place before, but to work, all of the elements had to fall into place. If previous attempts were made, obviously everything didn't click. But this Sunday night, all the pieces came together. **Bingo!** The perfect storm. Everyone's attention was riveted on the goal scoring action on the telly. Mr. Chase went to the WC. From the killer's position, he could see Giles leave and could see that the eyes of everyone else in the room were focused on the match on the telly.

The murderer moved over to the window behind where Mr. Chase had been sitting and opened it. I'm sure that Mr. Roche was as lax on locking windows as he was on locking doors, especially interior windows. The murderer then dumped the poison into Chase's glass, and quickly closed the window. The rest is history. It was a well-conceived plan."

"But who was that someone?" asked Roche.

"Well, what do you think, Sergeant? You have been studying this case along with me. You know the local constituents. Do you have any ideas?" asked Thompkins.

"No, not at this point. Not a clue. But then this is your show. I'm confident that you have some idea. Please continue."

"Are you sure you don't have any ideas?" She kept her eyes locked on his.

There was a pause . . . Sergeant Duke scowled, "What're you driving at Constable?"

"I think you know."

"What're you insinuating?"

"I think that someone was you."

A loud gasp reverberated through the room.

"That's absurd. Come on, I was home all night. I told you that. Constable, I think it is about time you backed off. I'm your boss, remember."

"If you were home all night, what were you doing?"

"Watching the football match, what else? I have had about enough of this idiotic rhetoric."

"Well, there is a big problem with your story. You see the night of the incident when I received the call from Dr. Brindley about the murder, our power at the station was off. I know, I was dying for a cup of tea. So today I went down to the power company. It appears that the big windstorm we had that night had downed a power pole that took out all power in the area around it. They also established the time when the power was out. It was during the last half of the match. Judging from the discussions that you were having with your colleagues here, and for not having access to a telly, you knew a whole lot about the second half of the match, the winning goal, and everything. I would say that you definitely saw it. Do you agree?

She continued, "But where did you see it?" Then pointing to the window behind Chase's table. "Through that window, there."

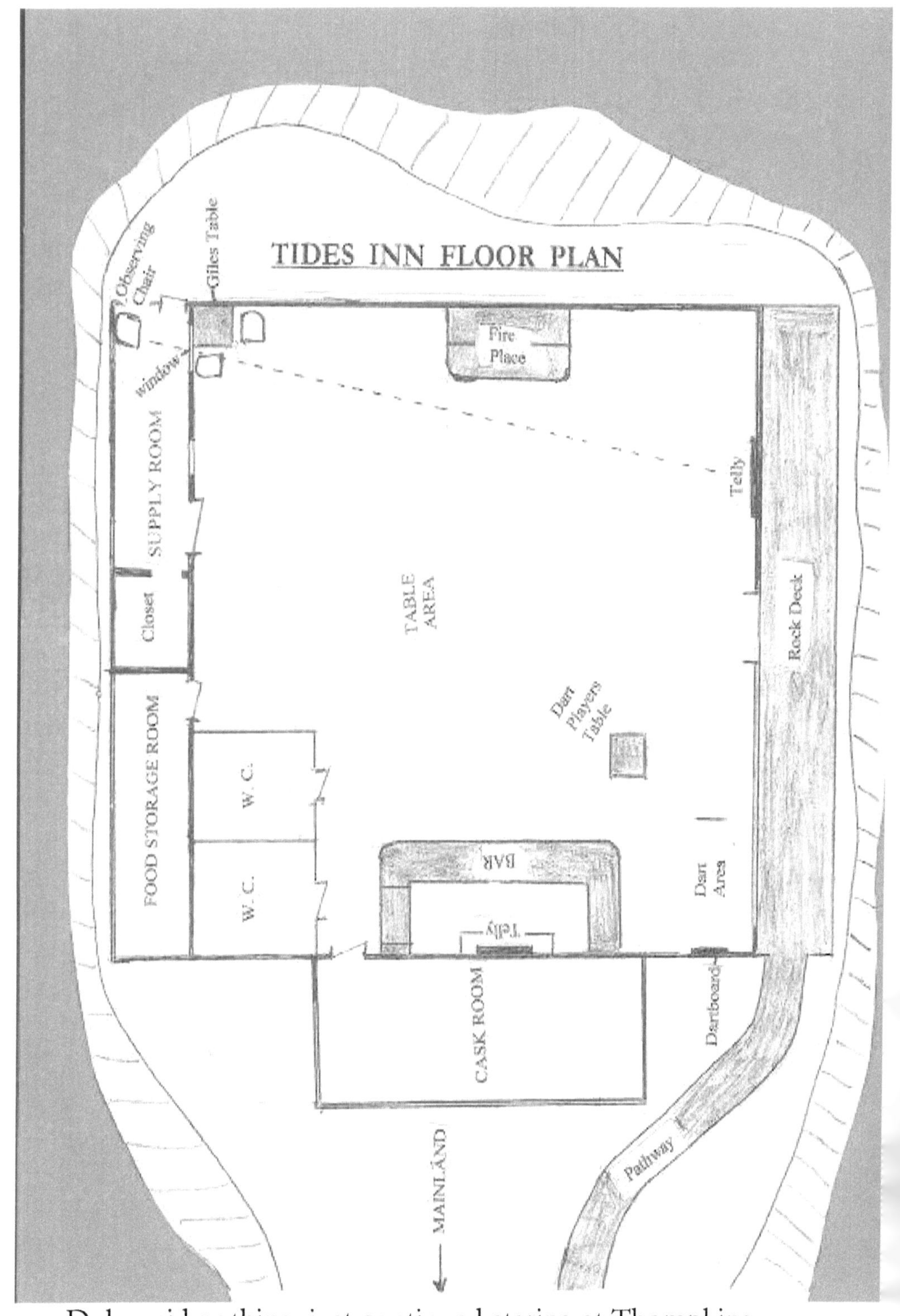

Duke said nothing, just continued staring at Thompkins.

"The power wasn't off at my place."

"Oh, I'm afraid that it was. The power company confirmed that your house was definitely in the area affected by that downed power pole."

"But how did you get Hamish's call, if the power was off?" asked Derek. "You need power to operate the telephone."

"As a police station, we can't afford to not have continuous telephone contact," answered Thompkins. "So we have a special battery pack as backup. Isn't that right, Sergeant?"

Duke just glared. After a pause, he asked, "But what would be my motive? I never had anything against Giles."

"Shall we say, blackmail?"

"Blackmail? What-the-hell are you talking about? Blackmail? Come on. Constable, you are out of your mind."

"Well, I know you think I'm some blonde bimbo that just walked in off the street. But you see in fact, I work for the Solicitor General's Office. We have had several complaints about some serious corruption issues here, some heavy-duty bribe taking. I was sent down to investigate."

"And have you found any wrong doings? Anything illegal?"

"No, I have not."

"Then what is your problem?"

"My problem is that I suspect that Mr. Chase had. He seemed to be good at this sort of thing, obviously better than I am. And he seems not to have had any qualms about trying to cash in on this talent. I suspect he was blackmailing you. You yourself said you suspected that he was indulging in this pastime. And in my book, eliminating a blackmailer is a pretty serious motive for murder."

She paused. Everyone still stared at her. She then added, "And you're very familiar with the Inn since I understand you helped Mr. Roche out quite often. I suspect you know every nook and cranny."

"But you yourself said you didn't find any evidence. How can you be so sure it was blackmail? You don't have much of a case there, Little Lady. Your evidence is all circumstantial. You don't have any kind of case that will hold up in court. They would laugh you right out of there."

"I'm afraid that would be true, except for one more little thing. One more mistake. You know that *Telegraph* that I found in the storeroom? The one somebody passed the time reading during that afternoon. I took it to the lab, and guess what they found? . . . Fingerprints. Fingerprints all over it. From the front page to the last page. Many people handled the paper before it was sold, so there were many different sets of fingerprints on the outside, but inside, where the prints would be of only the person who read the paper, the prints were of . . . only one person. The same person whose prints were on that cup of coffee that you ordered me to fix for you this morning . . . That person . . . was you."

A look of panic permeated the Sergeant's eye. He looked around the room. All eyes were staring at him. He gasped, whirled, and sprinted through the door, leaving behind a deathly-still room. No one moved.

Finally, Carole spoke up, "Constable, aren't you going to stop him? He's getting away."

"Don't worry, there're a couple of Scotland Yard Officers waiting at the end of the walkway. That is as far as his freedom is carrying him tonight."

"I can't believe it. He seemed to be a special policeman. A friend to all of us. I just can't believe it, I can't believe he murdered my Giles."

"That was almost a perfect crime, and was a perfect deduction," said an admiring Derek.

I can go home and tell my family about the very clever crime and investigation that I was witness to, Wow!" Said Ali.

"Constable, step up to the bar. You just earned a night's worth of drinking ahead, on the house," said Roche.

"Thank you, . . ." And then looking directly at him she said, "I think maybe I'll take you up on that . . . Gavin."

Gavin, his face glowing, returned with the beer, and put it down in front of her. "Here you are, Ma'am."

Carole raised her glass toward Thompkins and asked, "And what can we call you, Dearie? Constable seems so formal."

Again, looking directly at Gavin, Thompkins answered, "If this is my pub now, just call me, Dawn."

** THE END **

A TIDES INN MYSTERY

Book 2

Shock From the Deep

Bill Wilke

<u>SHOCK FROM THE DEEP</u>

Prologue

SUDDENLY a green figure explodes up in front of them. An arrow slices through the air. THUNK! A chilling, foreboding sound. The green figure disappears -- GONE -- in the blink of an eye.

Chapter One
--The Invitation--

Click – click – click. Sharp heels, attached to two pairs of black spit-shined shoes, belonging to two tall, black suited official looking men, resoundingly struck each of the 24 stone steps of a large official looking government building. Between these two men, being escorted, was a short dumpy middle-aged man, a large scowl pasted to his face.

At the same time, at the Tides Inn pub, twelve pairs of eyes intently watched the scene unfold, on the 'telly' above them.

On the 'telly' Elizabeth Thomas-Davie, an Investigative Reporter faced directly into the camera. "Mr. Brown certainly thought he was smart, and he was almost smart enough to get away with it".

The TV switched to a scene that showed the man being placed into a police wagon.

The camera split to John Fox, the commentator, and Elizbeth Thomas-Davie.

"Thank you, Elizabeth. As they say, 'when you turn Elizabeth loose, she gets her man'. I assume you have someone else in your sights".

"Yes John, we have two really hot situations going on right now. I'll keep you appraised."

Looking at Thomas-Davie, Fox responds "Two? That is interesting. Thank you, Elizabeth. We will be looking forward to hearing from you in the near future." Then looking into the television screen, "Yes folks, when our investigative reporter gets on the trail, the villains are in big trouble. . . Now to news on an explosion in Kent."

Everyone stopped paying attention to the telly. Discussions took place at the bar and in the dart area of the Tides Inn pub, a rugged, rustic building, built a short distance out in the sea, connected to the Yorkshire shore by a rocky walkway, subject to flooding, which occasionally shut down access.

Four of the patrons, who were absorbed in the TV proceedings, returned to their dart game: Derek Finnegan, in his early forties, an inventor and entrepreneur; Bunny Chase a widow, blonde in her thirties, who has retained her striking, ex-showgirl figure; Carole Coxton short, heavy set, buxom, peeking out through dark roots and stringy bleached blonde hair in her fifties; and Ian O'Brien, red hair, in his late thirties, with a strong brogue that accentuated his Irish heritage. A dart was thrown.

Lying on a chair, on a soft pillow in the corner was Mimi, Bunny's fluffy, white, miniature French Poodle. This was Mimi's home while Bunny was active in darts. Bunny cradled the dog in an over-the-shoulder front carrier when not partaking in a dart game.

Annabel Clarke, the bartender, in her mid-twenties, slim, attractive, very athletic, very short cropped dark spiky hair, strolled over to the backbar opposite where Hopkins Bay Police Sergeant Dawn Thompkins was seated. Tompkins was young, blonde, slim, attractive, tall about 6 feet.

Annabel asked, "Dawn, you know Elizabeth Thomas-Davie, don't you?"

"Yes, we were roommates at the University. Great lady."

"Have you seen her lately?"

"I hadn't seen her for several years but ran into her a couple of weeks ago. But we were both in a hurry. We promised to get together. But you know how that goes".

"Why put it off. Why don't you call her right now?"

"Well, I do have her card."

Dawn looked in her purse and pulled out Elizabeth's card. "I guess I could".

"There is no time like the present. If you don't do it now, when will you? Besides the weather is supposed to be good for a couple of days. Perfect for sitting on the deck, having one of Gavin's ales."

"You're right."

Dawn reached in and pulled her phone out of her purse and clicked off the numbers for Elizbeth's phone. The phone rang.

"Hello," answered Elizabeth.

"Hi, Elizabeth?"

"Yes, speaking."

"Elizabeth, this is Dawn Thompkins."

"Well, hi. What a surprise."

"I just saw you on the TV and your expose of Mr. Brown. That was a masterpiece. I'm really proud of you".

"Well thank you, Dawn."

"When we met the other day, we talked about getting together. Seeing you on TV tonight made me realize how much we do need to do that, and pretty soon. Do you think you could get away and come over here to Hopkins Bay? We could have a drink and a light lunch.? The weather is supposed to be good."

"Where could we meet?"

"The only place in Hopkins Bay is the Tides Inn. It is a picturesque pub, right on the water. Great ambiance, great beer, and the pub lunches are limited, as they have no kitchen, but very innovative."

"Oh, I have been there. That is perfect. Can't wait. This is a great idea. My doctor told me that I needed to get out of the big city for a while. A trip to the coast really sounds like what he ordered. And the thought of getting together after all this time sounds great. And I am familiar with the Tides Inn. I remember it was a great place to watch the sea and relax."

"When is the best time for you?"

"It would have to be on the weekend."

"How about this Sunday?"

There was brief pause.

"I just checked my calendar. Sunday will be perfect."

"One o'clock sound okay?"

"Perfect. See you then. Goodbye, Dawn, and thanks for calling. You are a godsend."

"Goodbye, Elizabeth."

Dawn shut down her phone and placed it back in her purse.

"Well," said Annabel, "it looks like you're all set. I will reserve the best table in the pub. And yes, the weather forecast is for warm and sunny, so I'll reserve one outside and one by the window, just in case the forecast misses."

Dawn returned to her drink and stared ahead.

The dart game became a little rowdy, and then became even more boisterous when Carole walked over to the dart board. "I DON'T BELIEVE IT! Three darts – two in the black bulls-eye, one in the red!"

"Three bulls-eyes," added Ian. "What a grouping."

Derek triumphantly walked over to the dart board. "We needed to close the bull-eye and 97 points to win. The red closed the bulls-eye, and two black ones give us 100 points. How about that?"

Bunny walked up for a closer look. "That is incredible shooting. Derek, you are incredible."

Ian added "And three po'nts to spare. Holy cow. That is impossible."

"I can't believe it myself," said Derek.

"Tht's ridiculous," added Ian. Then looking at Annabel behind the bar, he announced to the whole room. "Annabel, dr'nks for the whole room. Derek j'st pumped three darts into the bulls-eye, all in one throw."

Annabel was tending bar for Gavin Roche, the landlord of the Tides Inn.

After Annabel poured the drinks, Dr. Hamish Brindley lifted his glass in a toast, "Congratulations Derek. In all my years, I have never seen that happen."

Constable Edward Smythe, in his middle 20s who had just become Dawn's new assistant and was Annabel's boyfriend added from the bar, "Here – Here. I am totally impressed".

"O.K. everyone. You heard the man," said Annabel after all the drinks were poured, "As they say across the pond, belly up to the bar" Then adds, "I'm not bringing 'em to you.".

Sitting next to Constable Edward Smythe was Jacci Scott, brown tied-back hair, in her middle 30's, very attractive and athletic looking, who filled in as bar tender and food preparations at times.

The four dart players moved to a table adjacent to the dartboard. Ian walked to the bar and picked up four drinks. Then while he placed the pints on the table, "You deserve th's pint, Derek. And you don't know how much it pa'ns me to say that."

Derek lifted his glass, "Thank you Ian. That's very kind of you."

As she picked up her pint, Carole said, "Oh come on, let's not get carried away with this. You are making me sick.".

Everyone at the bar collected their drinks and went back to watching the telly.

A large glass cylinder filled with water with a dozen or so swimming goldfish sat on the far side of the room. A miniature sized stuffed diver floated on the surface.

All of a sudden, trumpets blared. The tank speaker was in action. Slowly the diver started sinking to the bottom of the tank. Bubbles escaped from bottom of his helmet. Eerie, bright lights in the cylinder started flashing,

Brice Loveridge, first time lodger at the Tides Inn, who was also standing at the bar jumped "WHAT THE HELL!"?

Annabel and everyone at the bar chuckled, "Sorry for the distraction. That gets everyone's attention the first time. The alarm signals that the path is all clear now."

Brice exclaimed, "That was quite a shock. Uh, nobody seems to be paying any attention to it."

Annabel explained, "All the old timers know all about it and are used to it. The little diver we call Ole' Pete. This whole show is a signal that the path is either opening or closing. When the tide is out, and the path is accessible, Ole' Pete lies at the bottom of the tank. Then as the tide comes in and the water outside starts reaching the top of the walkway, Ole' Pete starts slowly rising signaling that the water is starting to rise and the path to the mainland is shutting down, like now. Then everything is in reverse when the tide goes out. All the bells, whistles, lights and the trumpets accompany each change."

"Well, it is sure a big production."

"Yes, Gavin, the proprietor is big on the dramatics."

"Oh, and I might add that Derek Finnegan, the man over there that just hit the three bulls-eyes is the inventor of the system."

"That is pretty impressive. A man of many talents, huh. Since Ole' Pete is going down now, everyone can now escape."

"You got it," said Annabel.

"However, since I am staying here, I think I'll have another beer."

Annabel took his empty glass and turned to the beer taps.

Chapter Two
--The Get-Together--

It was a rare day at the Tides Inn, the water was calm, the sun was shining. The outside tables on the deck were brimming with customers enjoying the weather and good snacks and drink.

Seated at a table on the deck, overlooking the sea were Police Sergeant Dawn Tompkins and Investigative Reporter Elizabeth Thomas-Davie. With such a beautiful day, there were very few empty tables. The crowd at the bar included Constable Smythe, and Brice. The usuals, Derek, Bunny, and Carole, with Dr Brindley filling in for a missing Ian, were the foursome playing darts and watching the telly. Tending the bar were landlord Gavin Roche and bartender Annabel Clarke. There was a buffet of light food to feed those that that had an appetite.

Elizabeth's head suddenly laid back, her whole body quaked with laughter. "That was a riot. And Betty walked around the whole time not realizing what had happened. That was one of our better practical jokes.".

"Yes, it was, and we had some doozeys."

"Yes, those were fun days. I loved college."

"Yes, so did I. And you helped make it such a special time."

"Thank you, Dawn. And so did you."

They both were quiet for a few moments as each looked out over the sea reminiscing.

Then reluctantly returning to the present, Dawn made an observation, "Elizabeth, that blue sweater really looks good on you. It really brings out your blue eyes and your beautiful coal-black hair."

"Thank you, Dawn. I love the feel of wearing cashmere." Another pause, then Elizabeth said, "Changing the subject, I was wondering if you know Ian O'Brien?"

Dawn looks at her with a puzzled look. "Sure. He's one of our regulars."

Dawn then looks around the room. "I don't see him right now. Why do you ask?"

"Last time I was here I had lunch with him."

Just then Annabel arrived with another round, a beer for Dawn and a gin and tonic for Elizabeth. Small talk with Annabel followed.

"Annabel." Said Dawn, "I would like for you to meet my old friend from university, Elizabeth Thomas-Davie."

"Hi, Elizabeth. Very glad to meet you. I have been an admirer of yours. You have caught some bad people."

"Thank you, Annabel. This looks like a nice place to work."

"Good customers, good boss, good scenery. How can you beat working here."

Annabel then said, "Okay, I'll leave you two to your reminiscing.".

"My goodness," said Elizabeth as she watched Annabel walk away, "Our waitress sure seems to be in pretty good shape."

"Annabel is a top triathlon competitor. She takes off from work about once a month for a competition. She is always training."

"I can believe that. I wish I was in that good a shape."

As Annabel returned to the bar, she veered off to one of the corner tables, occupied by a tall black man, with close-cropped hair and well-fitting grey sweat suit. Everything looked normal, but if one had x-ray vision, one would see a firearm nestled in a shoulder holster under the sweat jacket. His steely, black, eyes expressed a focused interest on Elizabeth and her surroundings every moment.

"Would you like anything else, sir?"

The man was concentrating on Elizabeth. The question coming from right next to him startled him. "Ah . . . Oh yes, another sparkling water with lemon, please."

Annabel nodded, turned and headed for the bar again.

Both women leaned back, breathed in the fresh sea air and admired the view.

Elizabeth finally broke the silence. "Dawn, tell me about how you ended up here in Hopkins Bay."

"Well to make the story short, I was originally sent here to fill in a Constable vacancy on the local police force, and to look into some charges of corruption. Then, right after I got here, we had a rare murder, right here at the Tides Inn. I was lucky enough to solve it."

"Luck huh. I'll just bet."

"After that I was offered several promotions. One was to stay here with a raise to Sergeant. It was not a hard choice. I love this village, I like the job, and I have finally won over the people who live here."

"That is quite a success story. I am proud of you, Miss Thompkins."

"Well, thank you. That means a whole lot to me."

"How big a staff do you have here?"

"Well, after I was promoted up to Sergeant, it left an opening at Constable. Edward Smythe has joined me. He is young, 25, very inexperienced. Eager to learn. Sharp. Good looking kid. It's been fun training him. That covers my staff, not very impressive. Someday I will probably be ready to go on to bigger and better places. But right now, this is all I want."

"You do look very happy and contented."

"Yes, I am. Now what about you. I have been following your success as an Investigative Reporter. A very successful Investigative reporter I might add."

"Well, I do feel like I have found my niche. I have had some success."

"And some of that success was where others had failed, I might add."

"Well I have had some of that luck that you talk about too."

"Have you had any problem with threats and etc.?"

"Oh yeah, all the time."

"That must be nerve wracking."

"Well, it is at times. It also is sort of exciting."

"Do you have any protection?"

"Oh yeah. I have a bodyguard most of the time.

"Wow."

"In fact, if you look over at the table in the corner, the black man, with the grey sweat suit, that is Shawn Mitchell, a Royal Protective Squad retiree."

"Who is now Elizabeth Thomas-Davie's bodyguard." Added Dawn. "Wow, he does look pretty impressive. I wouldn't want to mess with you when he's around. I'm glad you do have protection."

"Yes, I feel pretty safe with him around."

"Now tell me about what cases you are working on."

"I really shouldn't, but since you are in law enforcement, and I know you will treat this as confidential, I guess I can talk a little about them. But obviously can't go into detail at this time."

Running her hand across her mouth, Dawn said "My lips are sealed."

"I have two going right now. Both of them I am getting pretty close to a solution, I think."

"Yeah, you mentioned the other night when you were on the telly that you had two cases lined up."

"Onc is an auto theft gang. They steal very expensive cars, strip them down for parts, and in even some cases combine them into very unique and fancy custom luxury cars."

"That sounds very inventive – and very lucrative."

"Yes, it is. And the boss of the operation, I believe, is a very unique man. His name is Neck Jackson."

"Neck?"

"Yes Neck. And for good reason. If you were doing a caricature drawing, you know what the dominating feature would be."

"Pretty thick neck, huh?"

"He tends to be different. Breaks from the norm. A famous, at least I guess in his world, bodybuilder."

"A bodybuilder?"

"That's what I said. I went out to interview him a couple of weeks back. What an experience. Large ego and sort of steroid crazed. Sometime when I have more time, I will give you all the sordid details."

"He does sound very interesting. I guess you could say he was up to his 'neck' in car thefts."

"Very funny," groaned Elizbeth.

What is the second case you are working on?"

"This one is also pretty interesting. His name is Pasty Douglas."

"Pasty? Where do you get these names?"

"Yeah, I know, you don't meet too many *Pastys*".

"He, also, like Jackson, is a handful to interview. Totally different from Neck. But different in his own way. When I went to interview him, the smoke about did me in. How he can survive chain smoking cigars, and existing in a nonstop smoke atmosphere is beyond me. And I don't think he is a very good person. He appears to be up to his ears in sex-trafficking."

"Sex trafficking? How is he involved?"

"Well, I am gathering information that indicates that he is forcing women, by various shady and illegal ways, into a prostitution situation."

"That doesn't sound very good."

"Sex trafficking is one of the biggest criminal businesses and is deemed the fastest growing criminal industry in the world. And it depends on men like him to keep it going."

"I hope you can put the kibosh on this as soon as possible. It is to your credit you have made it a target. That sounds very dangerous though."

"It has its problems."

Dawn leans back. "You do have an interesting job."

"Yes I do. Wouldn't trade for any other job on earth. And I plan on making it a very successful career. I have my sights set pretty high." Elizabeth looks down at her watch. "Oh my goodness. I didn't realize how late it is. I have to be going. This has been so much fun."

Just then Gavin walked by.

"Gavin", asked Dawn on his way by, "How does the tide look for leaving?"

"Probably about 15 or so minutes."

"I guess I'm going to have to wait 15 minutes then," said Elizabeth. Then after a pause, "I notice the way you look at Gavin. Something there?"

"Maybe," answered Dawn with a blush.

There is a silent moment when both women leaned back, sorry to see the visit about to come to an end.

Chapter Three
--Oh My God--

SUDDENLY a green figure explodes out of the sea. An **ARROW SLICES** through the air. **THUNK** – A chilling foreboding sound - the green figure disappears - Back into the water - **GONE** in the blink of an eye.

Paralyzed, Dawn stared at the lifeless Elizabeth, feeling like a sledgehammer had smashed into her body.

"ELIZABETH!" Everything happened so fast. She was unable to react. Tears rolled down her cheeks. An agonizingly few moments passed. Then her training and professionalism kicked in. She stood and moved over to Elizabeth, leaned over, placed her hand on her neck. No pulse.

People were screaming, running, diving under tables, rushing for the now tide-closed exit.

"Is she dead?"

Dawn looked up into bodyguard Shawn's eyes. "Yes."

"DAMN IT!"

Dawn rose up and with urgency in her voice said. "Go around to the other side of the building where you can see all of the shore in that direction. Watch for anyone coming out of the water."

Shawn took off running over the rocks behind the building to where he could get a good view of the shoreline on that side.

Dawn took out her phone and first called Edward who had returned back to the station. "Edward. A terrible thing has happened here at the Tide! Elizabeth has been killed. Get right over here."

She then called the medical services, knowing it was a total waste of time. She went to the exit rock walkway.

The water was still a little too deep to cross but appeared to be receding rapidly. She returned to the table where she and Elizabeth were sharing lunch, stared out at the sea and scanned the shoreline, looking for an assassin coming out of the water on her side of the building.

Gavin showed up at her side.

Tompkins asked, "How do we stand on the tide? Can I cross fairly soon?

"It won't be long. Just several minutes I think."

Edward called on her phone. "Sergeant, I'm at the end of the walkway. Do you want me to try to cross? It looks a little deep?"

"No, hang on. Wait there for now."

She continued viewing the shore, waiting for a glimpse of the exiting diver.

"Sergeant, you had better take a look at this."

She turned and looked up into the face of bartender Annabel. Annabel was reaching out, holding a pair of binoculars. Dawn grabbed the binoculars.

"Out there," said Annabel, pointing out to a specific spot in the sea.

Dawn directed the binoculars in the direction Annabel was pointing. After a quick adjustment she focused in on a sight that took her breath away. A green wet suited figure was crawling up the back of a boat, the *'MERRY LOO'*. The figure dropped into the boat's control seat. A rush of water emitted from the back of the boat, the motor roared into action, rapidly jumping forward. It headed for the end of a jutting point on the opposite shoreline, rapidly went around the point and disappeared behind the protruding land.

Dawn leapt into action. First, she called the Maritime Coastguard Agency. She alerted them to the crime and requested the Agency to have boats and planes out looking for the MERRY LOO.

She then dashed over to the walkway and surveyed the water situation.

Gavin walked up to her. Reading her mind he said, "I don't think it is quite low enough."

"No, I've got to go - NOW"

She sprinted to the side of the building and yelled. "Shawn, come here quickly!

Shawn hurried back to her.

Gavin said, "It is still too deep. It's too dangerous."

"I have to."

Shawn arrived.

"Shawn, we have spotted a boat which we are sure the murderer is using to escape. I'm going across the walkway to my car. Since there isn't any boat available. I am going to try to track him by land down the coast. I am deputizing you to take charge here. Get the names and addresses and phone numbers of every person here. And keep an eye on everything. I will be back to you later."

"Yes ma'am." After a pause, "Can you really deputize me."

"I'M DOING IT."

"Okay. Okay."

"Thank you."

She headed to the walkway.

Shawn called after her. "I assume Elizabeth must have told you who I am."

"Yes."

"I didn't do my job."

"No one did. No one could have."

As they walked toward the walkway Gavin said, "It is going down. I guess you do have a pretty good chance of making it, especially when I take you over."

"No. I have to take the chance before the boat gets away. But you don't. I can do it myself. I have to do it myself."

"Yeah, you probably can. But I am going with you."

"Okay. I don't have time to argue. If you're coming, then come."

Off duty, Thompkins was not in uniform. She wore a short skirt. Removing her sandals and placing them in the bag that hung over her shoulder.

Gavin passed her and grabbed a rail in front of them. "Here hold on to the back of my belt with one hand and grab the chain with the other."

He proceeded to wade ahead. They were doing just fine. The water up to their knees didn't seem like it was going to present too much of a problem. But then, out of the blue, a nasty whipping wave solidly blasted into them. They were not at a post when it struck, so they both had to grip on the chain with a one hand death grip, and tightly on each other with the other hand. Water was splashing up. The wave was trying to push the top of their bodies, and then pull the bottom of their bodies out to sea behind it. Then finally the wave started breaking up, losing its power and finally continued on empty-handed to the open sea. Thompkins and Gavin were left behind. They had survived.

As they reached the end, Dawn said, "Wow, where the hell did that come from."

"Yeah, I'm afraid we just crossed too early. When the water is still as high as it was just now, every once in a while, a sneaky wild wave like that will happen. If the water is below the top, it never happens."

"That is good to hear. Needless to say, I owe you big time, Gavin. Thanks!" A warm feeling came over her. Then looking at him she added, "Boy you are soaked."

"Don't worry, I'll wait a couple of minutes and when the water goes down, I'll go back to the Tide. I've got some warm, dry clothes in my room. I'll be all right."

Dawn's clothes were soaked, but she slipped on her sandals, and headed towards Edward's police vehicle standing right in front of the walkway.

Chapter Four
--Cut to the Chase--

She dashed to car and slide rapidly into the passenger side with Edwards behind the wheel

"Let's go," she screamed, while turning on the heater and directing the warm air flow directly on her.

With emergency lights blazing and horns blaring the car pulled out of the car park and headed south on the coastal highway. The car screamed along the road opposite where the outcropping jutted out into the sea. Thompkins stared out her window hoping to get a glimpse of the open sea, but her view was continually blocked by houses and trees. She was now too far inland. But, finally they broke loose past the jutting land and she was able to occasionally see through the homes and trees and get a glimpse of the water, but there was no cruising boat in sight. She was reconciled that the boat was well ahead of them, but she pushed Edward, "Faster! Faster! We have to catch up with it. I know, realistically I wasn't able to get away in time to do any good. But we don't have any choice than to try."

But catching up with it was not in the cards. After several miles they came to a turnoff to the Hopkins Bay Marina.

"Okay. We are not having any luck. Let's turn in here Edward and see what we can find."

They turned in just in time to see Ian O'Brien about to get into his car. Ian, one of the Tide's regulars, was the manager of the marina. He jumped several inches up and then dove around to the shelter of the back of his car as the racing, raucous car screamed into the car park. Thompkins and Edward jumped out of the car.

"WHAT T'E HELL IS GOIN' ON?" yelled Ian in his most panicky Irish brogue.

Dawn rapidly told him what had happened at the Tides Inn.

"My God! That is terrible!" he exclaimed.

"Have you seen any boats come in to the harbour in the last ten or fifteen minutes?" asked Dawn.

"Non'. I just came in myself . . . I did see a boat ga pas just outside the harbour entrance a short tim' ago."

"Which direction?"

"South."

"Where did it seem to be heading?"

"Hav' no idea. After it passed the entrance, I los' track of it. Had no interest, dont you know."

"And you never saw it again?"

"Na."

"Where were you with your boat?" asked Edward.

"Not my boat. I had an appointment to show one of the boats that is docked here that's fer sale. I do that on occasion for our dockers. But the potential buyers cancelled out at the last minute. I had it ready to go. I have been so busy lat'ly that I haven't be'n out in a while. The owners of this boat don't get out with it very often, so they're happy for me to take it out for a spin once in a while. This seemed like the idea' time to do it."

"Where did you go?" asked Edward.

"Just tok it out for a spin. Anchored it for a while, took off me' shirt, cracked op'n a couple of beers from the refrigerator, and lo'nged back enjoying the rare appearance of the sun. Very enj'yable to say the least."

"So that is why you weren't joining your mates in darts this afternoon," stated Dawn.

"Ay."

"I understand you knew Elizabeth Thomas-Davie."

"Ay. I did indeed. That is just terrible. Poor Miss Thomas-Davie."

"What was your relationship with her,"

"I didnt know her well. It seems that an acquaintance of mine in Ireland had h'r interest. At one time she had me down as a 'party-of-interest'. Every on'ce in a while, I understand she still makes a few inquiries into my involvement. It had somethin' to do with sex-trafficking. But I haven't heard much from her lately."

"Do you know a gentleman by the name of Pasty Dougal?" asked Dawn.

Ian paused, thinking.

"Ay. I have heard of him. In fact, Miss Thomas-Davie alluded to him several times in our conversations. But I can assure you that I do not know Mr. Dougal. In fact, I have never met the man."

"You said conversation'<u>s</u>'. Does that mean you met her more than once?"

"Ay. Once at the Tides, twice at her office."

"And you discussed only the sex-trafficking allegations?"

"Not allegations. There were no allegations. She just wanted information, which I didnt have."

"But she was interested enough to talk to you three times?"

"I told you I did n't have anyth'ng for her."

"This wouldn't go back to your IRA days, would it," asked Dawn.

Edward looked at her, puzzlement in his eyes.

"I guess - I guess that's always going to haunt me," said Ian. "No. The answer is no! Period."

"Well, I can assure you that this is certainly a concern. We will be searching very closely your connection with the IRA, and if it had anything to do with this."

"Ya won't find any. I assure ya."

"Okay. I guess this is enough for now." said Dawn.

"By the way," asked Edward, "Do you have a boat docked here named the MERRY LOO?"

Ian thought for a minute. "Na. No MERRY LOO."

"Do you know of any at all around here with that name?"

"Na."

Dawn asked, "Do you mind if we look around the decks and check some of your boats out?"

"Be my gu'st."

"Which boat is the one you were just out in?" asked Dawn.

Ian pointed toward one of the boats, "That one o'er there, the 'LEISURE WAY'.

Thompkins and Edward walked along all the docks, checking each boat. Some were tightly covered and wrapped and were immediately eliminated.

"What was this bit about the IRA? Where did that come from?" asked Edward as they walked.

"We had a case in the past in which Ian was one of our suspects."

"The case that you solved and were designated - Hopkins Bay heroine?"

"Well," Thompkins started to blush some, "That is exaggerating somewhat. Anyway, it came out that Ian in his younger days was involved with the IRA. He went to prison for one of his escapades."

"I have never heard this mentioned."

"Nope, and you probably won't. It ended up having nothing to do with the case, and we decided that since the facts in the case were confidential, that it wouldn't be mentioned outside the courtroom. It would have done nobody any good and made it unnecessarily tough on Ian. And if it does come up as important information, it is in the records and can be handily dug up."

"That is pretty nice of you. I know Ian must really appreciate it."

They then stopped at the 'LEISURE WAY', giving it a thorough search.

"I can't find anything out of order as far as I can tell," said Edward.

"Nor can I."

They finished their inspection of all the other boats, and unable to find anything of interest, returned to their police car.

"Well, what now?" Asked Edward as they drove off.

Dawn shook her head. "I have no idea. Let's go a little further."

Chapter Five
--Going Further--

They continued on down the coastal road, getting a variety of open views of the sea, but no boat.

"It doesn't look like we are going to have much luck. I wish I knew more about this area. We might as well turn back," said Dawn.

Just then, right on cue, a sign appeared, - "Hidden Cove Marina".

"Turn in here, Edward."

The car swung into a small marina, less than half the size of the Hopkins Bay Marina. There was no visual office, and no one around except for a woman cleaning one of the boats named the "SEA SCOTT".

She had her back towards them as they walked over to her. She turned.

"Well, hello, Jacci," said Edward.

It was Jacci Evans, part time bartender at the Tides Inn,

"Well, hi Edward . . . Dawn. What brings you out here?"

Edward explains the situation.

"That is just awful!" exclaimed Jacci.

Have you had your boat out today?" asked Dawn.

"Yeah, for a short cruise. It is such a beautiful day. Couldn't pass it up.   Got in some good meditation."

"Did you see any boats out on the water?"

"I didn't really notice. I was in my own world . . . Wait, there was one boat that went by. I sure do remember him. He was really flying. His flag was about to blow off, looked like it was ready to rip up. And his engine, it was roaring like a jet engine. Loud. Very loud. Very disturbing."

"Which direction?" asked Edward.

"South."

"Interesting,' mumbled Dawn. "What did he look like?"

"I don't really know. I didn't pay much attention. He had a muffler or something around his neck that was really whipping behind him."

"Are you sure it was a man?"

"No, could have been a woman I guess."

"Where did he go after he passed you?"

"I don't know. I just raised my fist to him as he passed, then I got back to my meditation. He wasn't around very long."

"Your fist?" grinned Edward.

"Well. It was some part of my hand," grinned back Jacci.

"Did any boats come in since you've been here?" asked Dawn.

"No, none."

"Okay, if you think of anything else, please let us know."

"By the way," asked Edward, "Do you know of a boat named "MERRY LOO".

"No, don't think so."

"None in the marina?"

"Nope. None that I know of anyway.".

"Okay. See you at the Tide," said Edward.

"Yeah, see ya. Bye, Dawn."

Dawn and Edward walked around the marina but found nothing suspicious and headed back to the car.

I don't think we're going to accomplish much driving around on land looking for a boat that is out on the sea. Back to the Tide."

Chapter Six
--Checking The Murder Scene--

Thompkins and Edward pulled into the Tides Inn car park, exited the car, and walked briskly down the now clear walkway. Most people were gone. The coroner was still checking the body. The deck was taped off with yellow crime scene plastic tape. There were no patrons left. Gavin and Annabel were still cleaning up. Shawn was still waiting for them.

"Find anything out there?" asked Shawn.

"No, nothing," answered Dawn. "What has happened here?"

"Everyone has cleared out. I've declared this as a crime scene. Don't know if I can do that but am going on your deputation."

"You're doing fine, Shawn."

"I have the names and have recorded the ID'S of all the people."

He handed the list to Dawn. They sat down with Edward at an inside table and went through all the information.

"That is strange", said Dawn while looking at the list. "There is a Mr. Duncan Taylor from Scarborough. That is where I grew up. I went to school with a Duncan Taylor. Is this a coincidence? Wow!"

Shawn, looking at the list observed, "Want more coincidence, the person below Mr. Taylor," Shawn points to the list, 'is also from Scarborough, a Mary Lou Taylor."

"'Mary Lou'! Oh my god!" exclaimed Dawn.

"When I was getting the ID information, I remember them coming through together. They were obviously a couple, probably husband and wife."

"I didn't notice them," said Dawn.

"No, I remember that they were sitting in a corner in the bar. Pretty much by themselves. Pretty lovey-dovey."

"Well, we 'will be doing a little investigating on that, for sure,' said Edward.

"Another thing, I noticed they were lovey-dovey, but he was on his cell phone a lot, to his wife's obvious irritation. Seemed to interfere with the lovey-dovey mode. Does give him a pretty good alibi."

"From doing it, but not from directing it. And he was on his phone a lot."

Shawn nodded his head.

They returned to scouring the list for further items of interest, but nothing else evoked their curiosity. So, they agreed that there was nothing more that they could do today, so they packed up to return home and to the station.

"Shawn," said Dawn, "We sure appreciate all your help."

"If I had done my job, you would not have needed it."

"Don't be tough on yourself. That was one clever murderer. None of us could have done anything about it."

"But that is what I was being paid for. I went through my whole career with the RPS and never lost anyone. Now my first client after leaving, bang, I lose them . . . And I liked her very much."

"Goodbye, Shawn. Again, thanks for your help and don't be too tough on yourself. "

They got to the car park and as they went to their cars, Dawn called to Edward. "Edward, be sure to contact the Maritime Coastguard and get a list of any registered boats by the name of MERRY LOO."

"Done,"

"Good."

Chapter Seven
--Putting Two Heads Together--

Thompkins and Edward meet at the police station.

"What do you have?" asks Thompkins.

"The report is back from the Maritime Coastguard."

"That was quick."

"It is very interesting. They say there is only one registered boat named the MERRY LOO on this side of the Isle. And it is in Scarborough. A man named . . . Duncan Taylor."

Thompkins stared at him. "Duncan Taylor?"

"Yep, that Duncan Taylor."

" Oh my god. I don't believe it! He was one of our gang. We all hung out together. I had a crush on him once. Elizabeth had a crush on him. Oh my god! We were at the university together . . . Find out his contact point. I'm going to go see him."

"Already done. He owns an automobile agency, 'Taylor's Elite Automobiles'. He specializes in fancy and expensive luxury used cars . . . Here's the address that is on his boat application. Looks like a business address."

Thompkins grasped the piece of paper and repeats, "Fancy expensive automobiles. That doesn't look good." She then grabbed the phone and dialed the number, gave her name, and asked to talk to Duncan Taylor.

After a pause, Taylor answered.

"Dawn Thompkins, the Dawn Thompkins, from school?"

"The one and only."

"Wow, what a surprise. What's up?"

"Well actually it is official business, though I would like to catch up on your life one of these days."

"What's the official business?"

"I'm a Police Sergeant in Hopkins Bay now and I am conducting an investigation."

"That wouldn't be about Elizabeth's murder?"

"Would you be available very soon? I would like to get together with you as quickly as possible. How about today sometime?"

After a pause, "Yes just checked my calendar. How about lunch?"

"I would like that, but I think since it is an official investigation, we should meet at your office."

"Okay, two o'clock. Do you know where my office is?"

"Yep, have the address and recognize the building."

"Yes, I guess you would."

"See you at two."

Chapter Eight
--The Past is Present--

As Dawn traveled down the A171, her mind went back to early, happy days, some of the happiest in her life. She and Duncan had some great times together - great times. She blushed when her mind settled on a few of those escapades.

She finally pulled into the town of Scarborough and pulled up to "Taylor's Elite Automobiles" complex. Among several large buildings was one housing the showroom and office. She went to the office and was ushered into Duncan Taylor's very plush office. Shiny wood polished furniture; soft beautiful, plush cushions; glittery brass and gold everywhere. Duncan had been very successful.

After exchanging greetings and a short nostalgic trip into the past, and Duncan's expression of sorrow over Elizabeth's death, they went into the business at hand.

"Duncan, I guess the first thing I would like to know is what were you doing at the Tides Inn when Elizabeth was murdered?"

"Mary Lou and I were celebrating our 15th anniversary. Hopkins Bay is one of our favorite get-a-ways. The "Royal Cliff" is one of our favorite hotels. The "Tides" is one of our favorite pubs. We go over there quite often. We were having a final drink before heading back home to Scarborough."

"Did you realize that Elizabeth and I were there.?"

"No. In fact, I didn't realize that it was Elizabeth until I saw it on the telly after we got home. We stayed away from the murder scene."

"Where was your boat?"

"Docked here at the Scarborough Marina."

"Could anybody have used it while you were gone?"

"I don't think so. No one else has access to it. Why are you interested in my boat?"

"We have reason to believe that it was used in the murder."

"My boat? Wow! I don't know how."

"We know a boat by the name, "Merry Loo" was used. And yours is the only Merry Loo registered on this side of the Isle."

"It is impossible! . . . My boat! . . . Impossible!. . . I guess someone could have taken it for the weekend while we were gone, I don't know."

"Have you seen it since you have been back?"

"Yeah. In fact, we stopped at the marina on our way home to drop some equipment off that we had purchased while we were gone. Hopkins Bay has a great boat supply store."

"What did you buy?"

"A depth finder. It is in the equipment locker."

"I see you deal in expensive used cars. Where do you get your cars to sell?"

"I have many sources."

"Do you have to rebuild them sometimes?"

"Yes, that is really our specialty."

"Where do you get the parts?"

"We have many sources for that also. And they are all legitimate, if that is what you are driving at."

"Do you know Neck Jackson?"

"He's that big body-builder isn't he. Yeah, I've heard of him, but I don't know him or have had any contact with him." Anger shaded his answer. "That seems to be a hidden accusation. I repeat, everything about my business is on the up and up, regardless of what this Jackson has done. And besides, what has that got to do with Elizabeth's murder?"

"Okay, I guess I have taken up enough of your time. I would like to check the MERRY LOO out."

"I have quite a few things going on right now. Could I send one of my salesmen with you over to the marina?"

"That would be fine."

Duncan asked his secretary to send over one of his salesmen to the entrance.

They walked out to the front door.

"By the way, Dawn, I don't know if you knew it, but Elizabeth had a reputation of throwing people under the bus to further her ambitions. She had a lot of bigtime enemies."

"That doesn't sound like the Elizabeth I know."

"No, nor of the one I know, but you should be aware of this in your investigations."

"I will Duncan. And by the way I'm sorry we had to renew things under these circumstances."

"Well why don't we plan on getting together after things clear up. Talk about the old days. I would like to introduce you to Mary Lou."

"Let's plan on it." said Dawn. "By the way, how did your boat get its name?"

"After Mary Lou. I was sort of kidding her naming the boat after her. but tweaking the name a little."

"Merry Loo --Happy Toilet? . . . You always did have a weird sense of humor."

Duncan grinned.

A glistening, transformed, black pickup, about three-quarters the length of a normal pickup, with front cloaked in a forest of shiny chrome grill, that looked like it had been squashed from both ends by a railroad locomotive pulled up. The smoky side window effortlessly sank, and a face peered out and received orders to lead Dawn to the boat at the marina.

Dawn bid him goodbye, walked out to the first row of parking, got into her drab blue police car, and followed the lead to the marina.

Chapter Nine
--Meanwhile Back at the Inn--

Edward entered the door to the Tides Inn, past an animated, lively dart game, and cozied up to the bar between Annabel and Jacci. He was off work and thirsty and longing for conversation with Annabel who was off duty tonight. Dr. Brindley was on the other side of Jacci.

"Hi Eddie," greeted Annabel.

Edward cringed with the 'Eddie', but grinned and bore it.

"Hi Annabel."

Annabel reached over and squeezed his hand.

Gavin was not occupied at the time, so he had Edwards ale out in front of him in seconds. The perpetually playing football match was radiating from the over-the-bar tally.

"Been looking forward to this ale all day."

"You look forward to an ale every day," said Jacci.

"Who's winning the match?" asked Edward.

"Liverpool," said Brindley. "How's your murder investigation going?"

Just then Ian, Bunny, Carole, and Derek, their dart game just ending, walked up and cozied up to the bar. Gavin turned to the beer taps behind him and started refilling glasses.

Edward continued. "Got lots of leads right now. You know we are looking for a boat named "Merry Loo". We found a boat with that name in Scarborough, owned by an old chum of the Sergeant, a man named Duncan Taylor. She went up to interview him today and inspect the boat. Didn't glean too much from either one. Boat was clean and there was nothing to connect him with the crime."

"Are you completely convinced that the "Merry Loo" was used in the murder.?" asked Jacci.

"Oh yeah. It is the vehicle."

"But at least you have a lead," stated Gavin, who was listening in behind the bar.

"That we do,"

"If this is the boat and the boatman you are looking for, I'm sure you and Dawn will find the truth," said Jacci. "Is that name really real? I mean 'Happy Toilet' or could be 'Slightly Drunk Water Closet'. I don't know which. I wonder how he came up with that name?"

"Well," explained Edward, "Sergeant said that he was teasing his wife with the name. Her name is . . ."

"Let me guess," interrupted Carole. "Mary Lou".

"You got it," said Edward. "Mary Lou."

"Now that is funny," said Bunny.

"But," continued Edward, "The interesting part about this is that he and his wife. . ."

"Mary Lou," interrupted Carole with a chuckle.

"Yeah, Mary Lou. They were here in the bar when it happened."

"In the bar!" exclaimed Jacci. "You got to be kidding.

"In the bar!" echoed Derek.

"Now that is weird," said Bunny. "What were they doing here?"

Edward answered, "According to Mr. Taylor they visit Hopkins Bay often, and they were celebrating their wedding anniversary."

"Come on, that's ridiculous," said Irish brogue Ian.

"Quite a coincidence," added Dr. Brindley.

"But at least they do have an alibi. Neither could have been our wetsuit murderer," said Gavin.

"But we think it is possible that it could have been Taylor's boat, and he could have been orchestrating the operation from the bar," said Edward. "It could have been an accomplice on the boat. Taylor was seen on his cell phone an awfully lot."

"Makes sense," said Dr. Brindley shaking his head.

"Do they have any kind of motive that you have come up with yet?" asked Bunny.

"Nope. None yet."

"I'm sure you will come up with something," said Annabel.

"What next," asked Jacci.

"Sergeant Thompkins

s is going up to Leeds to see a man named Neck Jackson who is, or rather was the target of one of Thomas-Davie's latest investigations and then on to checkout Thomas-Davie's office at the ITV station up there."

Things got quiet. Most eyes moved to the tally.

"Well, I think it is about time for another dart game," said Derek. Then addressing Edward, "Would you and Annabel care to get in on this one."

Both enthusiastically agreed and all six dart players headed back to the dart area.

Chapter Ten
--Muscle - Muscle - Muscle --

Police Sergeant Dawn was cruising along the A-64 toward Sheffield. The object of her travels, Neck Jackson, was according to Elizabeth, the object of one of her next exposes. After Elizabeth's description of him, Dawn was looking forward to meeting him. She entered Leeds and then followed her GPS down a tree lined path until she came to a pair of imposing wrought-iron gates, leading into a green well landscaped yard. Elizabeth had said he resided in a castle. The castle in front of her, though having stone exterior and several turrets was a little over named. It had the appearance of a castle, but was too small to actually earn the title, 'castle'. Though larger than a normal residence, mini castle would have been more appropriate.

Thompkins knocked on the door, then while waiting for an answer stepped back and surveyed the outside of the mini castle. The grounds, although not large, were well kept - lawn well cared for - bushes well-trimmed - stone exterior surface well maintained. Mr. Jackson was doing well.

A lady clad in plain cotton fabric housekeeper attire and wearing a small white cotton hat answered the door. However, the way she wore this apparel was not your normal, everyday housekeeper. The top three buttons of her top were unbuttoned, and the bottom of her skirt struggled to reach her knees, failing by 3 or 4 inches. Tucked inside this apparel, was a young, well-trimmed body. Thompkins was taken back. She recalled

Elizabeth saying that Mr. Jackson did seem prone to breaking from convention'.

"I'm Police Sergeant Thompkins," she said as she showed her credentials, "I'm here to see Mr. Jackson".

The young girl looked at the credentials. "Please wait here."

She left Thompkins standing at the open door. Thompkins again visually surveyed the impressive grounds. Everything orderly, green the predominate color.

After several minutes the maid returned. "Follow me."

Thompkins followed her through a sitting room and a long hall. The inside of the house complimented the outside, but a little gaudy. They reached a door. The girl opened it and entered a dark stairway that contradicted the rest of the house. Thompkins followed behind. At the bottom of the stairway, off to the right was another door. The maid took her coat, and Thompkins was ushered into a very large, basic room, cluttered with all kinds of weight and exercise machines. In a corner was a tanning booth. Centered at the back wall, with a window behind, was a large, ornate, carved wooden desk. Half-mooned in front of it were four large leather, over-stuffed chairs. Through the window, Thompkins could see a block wall rising out of sight, part of a basement rock wall well. A long wooden shelf at the side of the room, also similarly carved, struggled with the weight of a couple of dozen polished trophies, mostly gold.

Wearing a Tight "U" undershirt, Neck Johnson in his late 40s was in the last cycles of lifting a very sizable set of dumbbells. Muscles strained and quivered. A grunt emitted with each lift. A very sexual connotation was buried deep in each grunt. Printed on the front of his shirt was *'STUD'*, with *'Ultimate Body'* on the back. Nature and the weightlifting regime had produced a very short, stocky, almost grotesque body that appeared as wide as it was tall. Most of this stockiness was created by muscles layered on top of layers of muscles. Overhead lights reflected off the perspiration and through the wisps of steam that rose from the top of a glistening, round, shaved head, causing the underlying round-shaped face to appear even rounder.

As she looked at him a feeling of disgust passed over her. "Mr. Jackson, I am here to investigate . . ."

She stopped short as he whipped off his shirt, displaying a massive, bronzed chest, accentuating the weightlifting obsession and the triumph of the tanning booth. He grabbed a towel, wiped down the rolling sweat, and then draped the soaked towel over his bulging neck. A short, thick neck made it hard to tell where the neck stopped and the head began. Not hard to tell how he came by his name.

Sticking his chest out he said, "Pretty impressive, huh?" Then pointing his thumbs at himself, he added, "Ever see anything like this?" said with a mixture of intimidation and arrogance, "What do you think?" He then placed his hand behind his head and flexed the army of muscles.

Thompkins completely repulsed, and trying to overcome the intimidation, ignored the question. Holding up her credentials, "Mr. Jackson, I am Police Sergeant Thompkins. I'm here investigating the murder of Elizabeth Thomas-Davie."

Jackson took his turn ignoring the question. He walked over to the shelf behind his desk. He picked up one of the larger and gaudier trophies and started polishing it with the towel. "See this baby. Really impressive huh. I won it at the London English Weight-Lifting Championship. Look at this baby." he pushed it over in her direction."

Thompkins ignored it. "I would like to know what you know about the murder of Elizabeth Thomas-Davie."

Jackson, standing in front of her, pointed at himself, and asked, "Sergeant, honestly, have you ever seen a body like this?"

Thompkins just unbelievably stared at him.

After several silent moments Jackson, grinning, backed up, put his thumbs inside the top of his sweatpants. Then condescendingly said. "You really do like this don't you."

Thompkins jumped to her feet, rapidly stomped over to where he was standing. She towered over him. The contrast of a determined 6-0' slim, trim, statuesque body looking down on a 5-6 heavy-set fireplug, conjured up quite a comical contrast, sort of like a vison of a schoolteacher, hands on hips, soaring over a 3rd grade student. A *'DON'T GIVE ME ANY MORE CRAP'* look radiated from her eyes.

"LET'S GET THIS STRAIGHT *MR. JACKSON*. I am here for one thing and one thing only, to get information on Elizabeth Thomas-Davie's death. I AM not here to listen to the rambling of a steroid induced mouth. You can put some clothes on, NOW, and we can do this HERE, or we can do it at the STATION. It's your choice, but you had better decide fast because my patience is exhausted." She kept glaring down at him.

A stunned Neck looked puzzled. A 'what-do-I-do-now,' look shaded over his face. He finally turned with his back to her and gazed at the wall. After several moments he walked over and sat down behind his desk. Changing his attitude 100%, he looked at her and said, "Okay, Sergeant, what can I do for you."

"That is better Mr. Jackson."

He turned, scooted his chair over to a coat rack a little way away, grabbed a tee shirt off one of the racks and slid it on over his head.

"Elizabeth Thomas-Davie? And who is Elizabeth Thomas-Davie?"

"She was an investigative reporter for the Leeds Mail."

While talking he reached over to the side of the desk and picked up a hand gripper and started squeezing it. Throughout their conversation he rotated the grip workout from one hand to another.

"I never heard of her."

"That is strange. We have her notes from when she interviewed you. I doubt your memory is that bad."

"Okay, okay, I did talk to her once. Real pushy gal."

"What did you talk to her about?"

"Ah, she thought I was mixed up in some car stealing scheme."

"And are you?"

"What do you think. Of course not."

"You know Mr. Jackson, I feel like I have seen you before."

"Don't think so. Maybe you have seen me in one of my bodybuilding contests."

"Not much chance. Now, where were you at two o'clock last Sunday afternoon."

"Right here. I am a creature of habit and routine. I work out every Sunday from two o'clock to about four."

"And can anybody vouch for that?"

"Patty, my maid."

"She was here at that time."

"She is always here."

Thompkins leaned forward, her voice more intense, "Was Miss Thomas-Davie getting near the truth? Is that why you had to eliminate her?"

"If your scenario was true, then yes, that would have been a good reason for me to kill her. But your scenario is all wrong, I had no reason to kill her, did I? Besides, can you see me in a diving suit?"

Dawn tried to suppress the vision, but finally the humor of the sight broke through and her curled up lips betrayed her.

"Yeah, that would be quite a sight."

Neck grinned in triumph.

"How did you know about the wet-suit?"

"All the stories about the incident mentioned it."

"How could you read all these stories and then claim you didn't know her?"

"I told you, I did talk to her. I just forgot when you asked me before."

Dawn just glared at him for a few moments.

An uncomfortable Neck finally responded, "Okay, I made a mistake. Okay?"

"You certainly did."

"But I still could not get into the wet-suit you claim I was in."

"But you still could have been the mastermind behind this whole thing."

Neck put down his hand grips and with his eyes on the desktop did not utter a word. The intimidation factor had been reversed. For a few moments silence ruled the room.

Then Neck mumbled, "I didn't mastermind anything. Nothing at all. You got it all wrong."

Again, more silence.

"Okay Mr. Jackson. I guess that is all for now. But I plan on returning."

They both stood and walked to the door. Jackson opened it for her. "I look forward to seeing you again. Maybe I can show you a few things you've never seen before."

Thompkins's head swiveled at a high speed and gave him a scowl.

"Workout wise," he said smugly.

As she stepped through the door, Patty was there to meet her and helped her on with her coat.

As she started up the stairs, Jackson called behind her, "Oh, and I don't use steroids, I use legal supplements."

Thompson shook her head. Under her breath she said. "Whatever."

As the two women headed for the front door, Thompkins asked Patty, "Where were you last Sunday at two o'clock?

Without hesitation Patty answered, "Right here."

"And was Mr. Jackson here also?"

"Yes, I don't think he left the house the whole day."

She exited Neck's front door, feeling that she had just been through a surreal experience, got into her car, and headed toward the Lead's ITV station headquarters and Elizabeth's old office.

Chapter Eleven
--Darts and Gossip--

A furious dart game was resounding throughout the Tides Inn Bar Area. However, the participants were different tonight. Regulars Carole and Derek were joined by Edward and Annabel. Ian and Bunny were not there. But this has not decreased the competitiveness of the action. Jacci was tending bar while Gavin and Dawn were out to dinner. At the bar were Dr. Brindley and Elizabeth Thomas-Davie's private bodyguard Shawn Mitchell. The ever-present tally over the bar was presenting another action-filled football game.

"I don't believe I have seen you in here before," said Dr. Brindley to Shawn.

"Oh, I've been here a few times. I've just decided to completely retire and looking for a quiet place to settle down. Always have liked Hopkins Bay."

"And what did you retire from?"

"The protection business."

"Protection? In what way? Is it legal?"

Shawn laughed.

Just then the dart game came to a controversial conclusion. The dart players were moving toward the bar, and the unfair finish, at least in her eyes, was being loudly addressed by Carole. "that was just plain unfair!"

"What's the problem?" asked Jacci.

"They cheated," answered Carole.

"Always happens," chuckled Brindley.

"I think another round of beers will help soothe the pain," said Derek.

"Always works," said Brindley.

"Well, hello, Shawn," said Edward when he noticed Shawn. "What brings you here?"

"Just dropped in."

"Everyone, this is Shawn Mitchell. He was here during the incident and helped out big time."

"Yeah, I was telling Dr. Bindley here that I have decided to really retire and am looking for a quiet place to settle down. Always liked Hopkins Bay."

"Well, I'm pretty much a newcomer myself," said Edward. "But I like it here. I think you will too."

Just then a goal is scored in the football match. All attention is directed toward the tally.

After this action died down, Jacci walked over to Edward, "What's new with our case?"

"Well Sergeant Thompkins just got back from Leeds. She talked to one of the suspects up there, a very colorful gentlemen, a bodybuilder by the name of Neck Johnson. He was involved in one of Ms. Thomas-Davie's investigations. Then she went over to her office at ITV. Didn't find out much to help though."

Shawn tugged at Edwards sleeve and in a low voice the others could not hear said, "Edward, I don't think this is a topic that you should be discussing here. This should be treated highly confidential."

"Thank you. I guess I should have known that. It's just that they were all indirectly affected. And none of them are involved. Just keeping them up to date.

"Ian O'Brien is a suspect."

"I sure doubt he was involved. But you are correct. No more discussions on the subject."

"Good".

Just then Gavin and Dawn walked in.

"Shawn!" exclaimed Dawn. How good to see you."

"Yes, Mr. Mitchell is staying here for a few days," said Gavin.

They were asked about their evening and Gavin went on to answer them. Dawn, on the other hand slid in next to Shawn.

"What are you doing in Hopkins Bay?"

"Just looking for a place to settle down in my retirement."

She looked at him. "Retirement? That is too bad . . . but very understandable. I can imagine what you are going through.'

"Yeah. I have been considering this for some time. I just need to do it right now."

"I have to ask, why here? It seems like it might be hard to deal with."

"Yeah, you would think so. I don't know. I have always liked this area, I like this pub. It seems like the people are nice here. I have been accepted here. I don't know, despite the memory, or maybe because of it, I seem to be drawn to it."

"Well, I am glad."

The evening continued with lively banter until Ole' Pete's sound and light show finally broke the evening up and all went to their night's dwelling.

Chapter Twelve
-Where There Is Smoke -

Dawn entered a long circular driveway, stopped at the front of an elegant front door of a luxurious large mansion, got out, walked to the front door and rapped on the door with a very ornate brass knocker. A very shapely, well-dressed young woman answered.

"Yes?"

Dawn handed the door lady her credentials and said, "I am Police Sergeant Thompkins. I would like to see Mr. Dougal, please."

"And can I tell him what this is about?"

"I have to see him on a police matter."

The door lady shrugged her shoulder. "Please wait here."

Taking the credentials with her, she disappeared, then returned shortly. "Please follow me."

Dawn thought, "Two large mansions in two days. This case sure reeks with money."

They walked by a large indoor swimming pool, decorated with five revealingly bikini dressed and undressed, well-endowed young women lounging by its side.

They came to a large wooden door. Her escort knocked.

A voice boomed, "Come in."

They entered. Thompkins was immediately engulfed by heavy, dark smoke, and overwhelmed by its smell.

Thompkins first thought, 'The place is on fire.' She was in dire need of a respirator. She would even settle for a fire extinguisher at this point.

Sitting behind an impressive mahogany desk, engulfed in his cloud of smoke, was Pasty Dougal, in his 60s. Very expensive Gucci shoes were propped up on its top, soles pointed directly at her. Dougal's entire attire exuded extravagance. A plethora of silver-grey, wavy, thick hair, every strand perfectly in place, embellished the top of his head.

"He must have a very thriving hairdresser," she thought.

Dougal was speaking on the phone. He motioned for Thompson to sit down. The conversation was with a man named Bull and involved some business deals. He continued puffing on the cigar. The smoke continued to really irritate her, both physically and psychologically. Finally, after keeping her waiting for the proper amount of time, he finally hung up. Before he said anything, he expelled a puff up in the air away from her, but not surprisingly the air draft carried it right back into her face, triggering a flow of tears.

"Mister Dougal, can you please put that cigar out until we are finished."

He inhaled one more draw, held it for a moment, then again exhaled, and looked at the smoke admiringly, as not surprisingly, the smoke followed the same path. He squashed the cigar in an oversize, gaudy, weighty marble ashtray and placed the dead stogie back in his mouth, gripping it in his teeth. The dead cigar smell left her with a churning stomach. The smoke mostly finally drifted away, but the obnoxious smell lingered on.

"Okay, Little Lady, what can I do for you?"

"First off, you can call me Sergeant. Secondly you can answer some questions related to the murder of Elizabeth Thomas-Davie."

"Ah yes, Elizabeth Thomas-Davie. Around here we call her bulldog. That was quite a shock. Who would want to kill her?"

"Well, from what I have learned, you would."

"And why would I want to do that, Little Lady."

"Please . . . SERGEANT!" She paused, then continued. "Because she was investigating your involvement in a sex trafficking scheme."

"You're not serious are you?"

"Very serious".

"Those are strong accusations. I hope you can back that up."

"Where were you last Sunday around two o'clock."

"I was out on my boat."

"And what is the name of your boat?"

"The HAVANA KING".

"Really? Why HAVANA KING?""

"That's the only cigar I smoke. So if you want to give me a gift, that is it."

"I'll keep that in mind."

"Can anybody collaborate your story?"

"An alibi you mean. Yes, there were several of my business associates along."

"Could I have a list of them?"

He picked up the phone. "Jennie, look in my appointment book and type out a list of people that were on the boat with me last Sunday."

Then addressing Thompkins, "Okay, anything else. I have some important meetings coming up."

"I'm almost through. Where did you go."

"On our little cruise? We just went cruising up along the coast."

"South or north, and where did you start from?"

 "South from the Hopkins Bay Marina."

"Is that where it is docked, and how long were you out?"

"We were out from about 1:30 to 5:00. And yes, that is
where it is.
docked . . . How would you like to join us next time? We have an exceptional bar onboard, and the food is always first class."

"I just bet it is, and no thank you."

"All I can tell you, <u>Sergeant</u>, is that Bulldog was way off target and there was nothing she could find out about me, so there is no reason for me to eliminate her. I did not kill her!"

Thompkins felt good about the emphasizing of Sergeant but winced at the Bulldog reference for Elizabeth. "Did you have her killed?"

"No! I do have an urgent appointment now. If there is nothing else, I would like to end this charade."

"One last question. Do you know an Irishman named Ian O'Brien?"

"Never heard of him."

"Are you sure? He knows you."

"If I ever knew him, I have forgotten him. Must be pretty insignificant."

"How about one of your trips to Ireland."

"Why would I want to go to Ireland?"

"To meet with Mr. O'Brien?"

"Oh, come on."

"How about at the Hopkins Bay Marina?"

"This is getting ridiculous, Little Lady. I'm through."

"Okay Mr. Dougal. But I will be back."

"You're always welcome, Little Lady."

Thompkins cringed and then stood up. Her stomach started churning again as the smoke smell floated even stronger at the slight rise in altitude. She started for the door.

Dougal got up, moved ahead of her to open it and held it open for her. Jennie met them at the door and handed Dawn the list of names she had requested.

"There you are Little Lady."

She cringed again, shrugging her shoulders in surrender. "Thank you."

As they walked away, headed for the front door, Dougal called out behind her, "You wouldn't like to work for me, would you?"

Dawn turned to look at him, "No thank you, Mr. Dougal. I think I would rather work in a sweatshop."

He grinned, satisfied that he had succeeded in getting to her.

Dawn and Jennie continued on to the front door.

Chapter Thirteen
--A Major Goof-Up—

The next evening found Dawn and Edward at their desks studying files.

"So," asked Edward, "How did your meeting go with the 'gangsta'?"

Dawn chuckled, "Very interesting to say the least. He is quite a domineering human being. He certainly appears to have the personality to plan a murder, but I don't think he was capable of getting a wetsuit on and actually carrying it out . . . Oh, and he offered me a job."

There was a pause as Edward continued looking at the papers in front of him. Suddenly his head flew up. "What? Doing what?"

"He didn't elaborate, but it would have been something illegal, I'm sure . . . And interesting."

Edward chuckled.

"So," said Dawn, "Let's see what we have. First there is this Mr. Dougal. It looks like Elizabeth was about to expose Mr. Dougal's sex slave operation. By all appearances, it looks like it is doing well by him. She probably was getting close to closing the deal on him. But it looks like he might have managed to quiet that investigation for now."

"A good prospect, but we need a lot more evidence."

"And what about Ian's connection with him. It seems odd that Elizabeth would be interested in both Dougal and Ian while investigating a sex operation. I just can't see Ian involved. I guess it could have something to do with the IRA."

"Yeah, could be, I guess. What about your old boyfriend, Duncan Taylor?"

"I don't know. I can't see any connection between him and Jackson. It seems like right now we are with four parties of interest."

"Yes, with two each of our suspects possibly strangely linked together to two entirely different operations. . . Dougal and Ian could be linked together in the sex operation."

"And," added Dawn, "Jackson and Taylor linked together in the car stealing operation."

"Yes, in this case, Jackson steals them, strips them, and fixes them up, and Taylor sells them. Could work out well for all parties."

"But if you had seen him, you would know that there is no way Jackson could have ever gotten a wet suit on over that grotesque body."

Edwards chuckled at the vison.

"And Taylor was in full sight in the pub during the murder."

"Talk about an air-tight alibi."

"However, there is no reason that one or more of them didn't plan the whole thing."

"Yes, it looks like we don't have a shred of evidence at this point."

"And then maybe none of them are connected at all."

"Well," said Dawn. "Somewhere in Elizabeth's files there has got to be the answer."

They both then returned to their files.

Dawn, while still bent over the files said "Sorry to keep you tied up tonight. I know you would much rather be with Annabel instead of here."

"Nah, she is over at Jacci's for a girl's night out - cocktails and dinner and all".

"Well, hopefully we won't have too many more night investigations."

*　*　*

A knock at the door. Jacci answered.

"Hi Annabel. Come on in."

"I'm really looking forward to our little get together."

The table was all set, the smells, a result of a well put to work kitchen, with hints of what was to come next, wafted in the air.

"It sure smells good in here," said Annabel.

"Sit down. The champagne is chilling."

"Before we start, I have to text Eddie."

"Why do you insist on calling him Eddie? He hates that name".

"It's just a tease."

Jacci just shook her head.

Annabel texts the message using vocal directions. Holding the phone up to her mouth: "Eddie (comma) I am now at Jacci's for cocktails and dinner (period) Hope you don't have to work too late (period) Love (comma) Annabel."

Annabel then pressed the send button. But in pressing it, the phone flipped in her hand and flew up in the air. She fumbled with it as it bounced around in her hand until she finally controlled it, and then put it down on the living room coffee table.

"Wow, that was impressive," exclaimed Jacci. "That phone was all over the place. Great grab."

"Yeah, just about dropped it."

They then sat down around the coffee table. "Okay," Jacci popped the cork and poured the bubbly into champagne glasses. Raising her glass, she started her toast, "now for this toast to our night to celebrate." . . . and then continued the toast.

*　*　*

Meanwhile back at the station, Dawn and Edward are buried in the files of the case. **"DING"**. A text from Annabel appeared. Edward looked at it.

"Who is that?" asked Dawn.

"Annabel. She says she loves me and wishes I was there."

"Lucky guy. I know you would rather be there too."

"Nope, I'm fine. I am finding some interesting stuff on your boyfriend, Pasty Dougal."

Dawn frowned at 'boyfriend'.

"Let me know when you're finished. We can go over that and some stuff I have gathered on Neck."

"Neck. My, we are on first name basis now, huh?"

Dawn gave him a dirty look and then went back to her papers.

*　　*　　*

Later Annabel and Jacci finished the champagne and dinner and started to move back to the living room. As Annabel sat down, she looked at her phone and then picked it up.

"Whoops, I guess in my fumbling around with my phone, the message I sent to Edward didn't go through like I thought it did. My message is still waiting to be sent."

She presses the send button.

Jacci went to the liquor cabinet, grabbed an expensive bottle of port and a box of chocolates, sat down again and placed the delicacies on the coffee table.

"Wow," exclaimed Annabel. "That is expensive port."

"The occasion warrants it, don't you think."

"Absolutely."

*　　*　　*

Meanwhile, back at the police station Dawn and Edward were still buried in files.

"DING". Edwards text message signal went off again.

"My she must REALLY love you," teased Dawn.

Edward grinned as he picked up the phone. He read the text. The grin vanished. Blood drained from his face. He stared out into space. He sat stunned. After several moments he went back to his phone, slowly rereading it, digesting every word. Stared into space again. He then got up, feeling weak, walked over to Dawn's desk, and placed the phone in front of her.

"You'd better look at this."

Dawn read the text. She too then stared into space. After a short time, she got up, slammed her notebook down on her desk, "Let's go."

She headed for the door. Edward's right behind.

Chapter Fourteen
--The Truth Be Known –

Dinner liqueurs were finished. "I guess it is time for me to leave. It has been a special victory celebration," said Annabel.

Just then there was a knock on the door. Jacci got up to answer it, and as she headed for the door, she looked back over her shoulder. "I would say that we lady avengers did a pretty good job."

"Daddy would be proud," answered Jacci.

Jacci answered the knock at the door, "Well, hi, Dawn - Edward." A slight look of puzzlement took hold of her face.

"Can we come in?" asked Dawn.

"Of course." Still puzzled.

And as they entered Dawn asked, "And could we see Annabel's phone?"

"I guess so . . . Annabel, okay?"

"Well, yeah, I guess so."

Jacci walked over to the coffee table. Returning with the phone, her attitude changed to a slight show of fear as she handed it to Dawn.

"Why do you need my phone?" asked Annabel.

Dawn did not answer. She handed the phone to Edward. He immediately started pushing buttons.

"Dawn and Edward joined the women in the living room but remained standing.

"Do you have it?" asked Dawn.

"Got it," answered Edward.

"Read it.

Edward proceeded to read:

> *"wow that was impressive that phone was all over the place great grab yeah just about dropped it ok now for this toast to our night to celebrate us the lady avengers justice has been served it is too bad daddy isn't here but i am sure hes looking down from heaven rejoicing that revenge is finally ours daddy can now rest in eternal peace that evil woman is gone the lady avengers have struck and a thanks to eddie for keeping us up to date on the investigation again here's to our perfect crime with that arrow from the deep justice has been done the witch is dead"*

Edward stopped reading the text."

There was a long silence.

Edward broke the silence, "Notice that there was no punctuation in the last part of the text. Which means this part must have been sent by vocal instructions, without knowing, and without punctuation added."

Dawn added, "Which means the phone accidentally picked up its instructions from the discussion in this room. A very interesting discussion, I might add. It certainly wasn't intentional.

Again silence.

Dawn ended the silence, "Well ladies. I think your perfect crime is no more. I have to give it to you, you came up with quite a plan. It was almost perfect."

"Almost," chimed in Edward. "We never ever suspected you.

Jacci, in a low, sad voice, "That woman was evil. She framed our father for murder – a murder he never committed," (her voice rising) She fabricated the crime, dug up false evidence. She stood by and allowed our father to be executed."

"Just to advance her career. Even though she knew her evidence was false, and he was innocent," broke in Annabel. "She was evil."

"Okay, it is time to take you both down to the station," said Dawn.

"Edward," declared Annabel, "I am sorry the way things have worked out. I do love you. If only this opportunity for revenge hadn't come up, I think we would have been happy together. You are a great person. But our family has a history of loyalty".

"WE HAD TO AVENGE OUR FATHER!" cried Jacci.

Chapter Fifteen
--What a Plan –

Dawn and Edward walked into the Tides Inn.

"All hail the conquering heroes," exclaimed Carole.

"Hear, hear," called out Derek.

"Tell us what happened," said Bunny.

All the regulars were there. Gavin, Brindley, Derek, Carole, Bunny, Ian, and Shawn.

"Yeah, come on up, the drinks are on the house," proclaimed Gavin.

"Ya, tell us," said Ian.

"As soon as we get our drinks," said Edward.

"You always did have priorities, Edward," chided Carole.

The drinks arrived and Dawn started off, "I guess since it is all solved, we can share some of the details."

Dawn described the scene. "The activity on the deck had quieted down some. Because of the tide cutoff, everyone had been served and no new customers were able to come in. So, Annabel was able to sneak away to the backroom. There she quickly donned the green wetsuit, exited the backdoor, slipped into the water, swam underwater around the end of the building, to right in front of us, popped out of the sea, fired an arrow, then quickly submerged again. She then returned underwater to the back door, exited the water, went back into the storeroom, changed out of the wetsuit, returned to the pub."

Edward then took over. "In the meantime, Jacci hung a MERRY LOO sign on some added hooks on her boat covering the 'SEA SCOTT' name. Wa lah, we now have the 'MERRY

LOO'. She then anchors it offshore in sight of the Tides Inn, dons an identical green wetsuit, goes into the water and waits. At a phone signal from Annabel, telling her that the boat is in view of Dawn's binoculars, Jacci climbs back up onto the deck, starts up the engine and guns off around the corner of the outcropping, out of sight. As soon as she is out of sight, she rips off the sinkable sign and the suit and tank, and dumps everything overboard, the wetsuit being weighted by the tank, and hightails it on to her own marina."

Dawn then broke in again. "After Annabel had shed her gear and placed everything behind several preplaced big boxes, she left the storeroom and went straight to the back of the bar. On the way she messaged to Jacci's waterproof phone that it was time to enter the water. Jacci did just that, waited several minutes then climbed back into the boat. When Annabel got to the bar, she grabbed the pair of binoculars that Gavin always kept there and ran over and handed the binoculars to me and pointed toward the MERRY LOO. I caught Jacci in the binoculars just as she was surfacing. She then started up the boat ladder. I saw an identical wetsuit. The same color, everything. Obviously, 'The Murderer''. It seemed so logical. The murderer - no doubt about it. I fell for it completely.

There were several murmurs from the gathered crew.

'We had several suspects, as you know, said Edward, "But we never in the world suspected Annabel and Jacci."

Shawn asked, "How did you nail them?"

Dawn answered, "I hate to admit it, but it was a fluke. Annabel and Jacci were having dinner together. Annabel sent a text to Edward. While trying to send the text, she fumbled the phone. While trying to corral the out-of-control phone in the air, she did actually press the 'send' button and the message was sent. But she didn't realize it. And in the process, as she continued fumbling with it, she pressed the Text Message and Voice Activation buttons again which activated it once again, a second time for a second text. She put it down on the living room table, thinking she had sent the message, which she had, but not realizing she had also activated the text button again?

Edward took the stage, "Jacci then presented a toast that bragged about how they had avenged Ms. Thomas-Davie, incriminating themselves big time. This was picked up, interpreted, and printed out by the phone's vocal text. Annabel later glanced at the phone and saw that a message was waiting to be sent. She thought that it was her first message and it had not gone. So, in pressing the send button, she thought that she was sending the first text, but in reality, was sending the second incriminating text. We had enough of a confession to nail them."

Derek asked "But, the timing has me confused. By the time Annabel donned her suit, entered the water behind the Tide, swam around to you two, fired the arrow, came back to the rear of the Tide, removed her suit It seems like too long a time. Especially the wetsuit on and off."

"Remember," answered Dawn, "Annabel was a big-time triathlon participant and was world-class in the swimming part. So, the swimming part didn't take very long."

"And," jumped in Edward, "A triathlon racer is very adept at getting out of a wetsuit fast after the swimming portion of the race. It is essential. Time can cost them the race. A triathlon racer knows all the tricks. I checked. They shoot for no more than 20 seconds to get out of their suit. And Annabel was an expert at this. And she has put the suit on so often, she knew all the tricks to do this too."

Now it was Dawn's turn to jump in. "And, it only took an instant to come out of the water, fire the arrow, and dive back into the water. So, the whole operation happened fairly quickly."

"What happened to the equipment?" asked Ian.

Dawn answered, "She used the back storeroom to operate in. As I mentioned before, when she returned from her swim, she stashed everything behind a bunch of large boxes that she had made sure were there, came back after dark, loaded everything in a large gunnysack and threw it out in the water. The tank was heavy enough to weigh everything down. She told us where she dumped them, and we had a diver go down and find the bag."

Edward broke in, "Annabel told us that they had practiced this whole scenario several times and felt that they had everything down pat."

"Did they use an underwater speargun?" asked Brindley."

"No," answered Dawn, "They used a short stock crossbow. A spear gun is not accurate or practical enough to use out of water. And this cross-bow can be submerged in water without any adverse effect and brought up and launched immediately in air."

Explained Edward, "It appears that Annabel has had training on this type of bow.

"And," added Dawn, "it should be noted, that Annabel's close cropped, spiky hair was perfect for the plot. One quick toweling off, and bingo, no more noticeable wet hair.

Shawn commented, "They seemed to have thought of everything."

"Everything," said Carole. "but an eve-dropping telephone."

"And another of the many surprises that we have been hit with," added Dawn, "is that Annabel and Jacci were sisters. Jacci had been married before. Her maiden name was Clarke, like Annabel, but she married a man named Scott, which she kept.

"And," added Edward, "they managed to keep secret the fact that they were sisters."

"That is amazing, said Gavin. "You think that you know someone, but you really don't.

"How true," said a very sad Edward.

"Great work," complimented Dr. Brindley.

Dawn modestly answered, "Not necessarily. They basically nailed themselves".

Edward added, "It was close to being the perfect crime."

Gavin added, "Oh, you would have gotten them, one way or another. I have no doubt."

Dawn looked at him affectionately.

Carole walked over and gave Edward a big hug. "Edward, this must be very rough on you."

"You know there is one troubling aspect to me though, "said Dawn. "If they are right about Elizabeth, that is very disturbing. I know Elizabeth was an extremely ambitious, woman but to do this, I just can't believe it."

"Yeah, I can see where Annabel and Jacci might be driven to revenge,' commented Derek.

"Yes, it is very disturbing." Said Dawn.

Edward said, "After hearing their story, I am sure they believed it was true."

"Maybe if they can prove it, it might help them some way or the other in their legal fight," added Brindley.

"I think Edward believes that also," said Dawn. "He has taken next week off and plans to investigate what he can find out and if there is any truth to their story.

"Yes, I did really love her. I still can't believe it," said a remorseful Edward.

THE AUTHOR

Bill Wilke spent much of his life working all over the world. Nineteen of these years were spent in the Middle East; one in Saudi Arabia; three in Jordan; eleven in Egypt, which was under the rule of a dictator, President Mubarack at the time; and four years in Libya, under a dictator, Colonel Khadafy. Being a part of the culture for this period enabled him to get to know the people and their mind-set and customs and appreciate them. It also allowed him to observe the good and the bad of a dictatorship government. This has provided the inspiration and the foundation for another book entitled Doublestar *Conspiracy*. (See below.)

He has also written a children's book, *Maadi's Adventures in Egypt,* based on his 11 years, and Maadi's 6 years in Egypt, the center of the world's greatest antiquities.

He attended Louisiana State University, is now retired and residing with his wife Sally in the Lake Tahoe, Nevada area.

Join him at: Website: www.billwilke-international.com
Email: bswilke2@gmail.com

<u>Two other books by Bill Wilke:</u>

1. <u>DOUBLESTAR CONSPIRACY</u>

Terrorist or Freedom Fighters

**Action-Packed . Thought-Provoking . Conscience Challenging.
Difficult and Painful Life and Death Decisions**

<u>Four groups -</u> a ruthless foreign dictator - a group of dissidents out to save their brutalized country - a couple who while on a camping trip accidentally witness an assassination attempt - and innocent people who are not aware that they are being drawn into an deadly conspiracy - all heading into an explosive collision.

<u>Terrorists</u> have had to resort to <u>terrorism</u> to eliminate <u>terrorism</u> in their decimated country.

Does the end justify the means?

■■

2. MAADI'S ADVENTURES IN EGYPT: (a Children's Novel and also Dog Novel)

Maadi's Adventures in Egypt deviates from the norm. Exotic Egypt is brought to life through the eyes of a mischievous, adventurous, lovable, canine named Maadi. It is not just a travel book. It is not just a geography book. IT IS a fun book that will educate and entertain, while bringing the sights and culture of Egypt alive. It is an exposure to a different culture. It is a study of Maadi's relationships with humans and dogs alike of all different cultures and nationalities – all wrapped up in an entertaining, educational, and inspirational book, brought to life with over 50 photos and maps, with a chuckle or two along the way. Maadi resided in Egypt and the Middle East with her owners for six years. Many of her adventures in this book are founded on real life experiences.

(Warning - Grownups may also find this an entertaining and enjoyable read.)